BURNING KISS (SPECIAL FORCES: OPERATION ALPHA)

AIR FORCE FIRE PROTECTION SPECIALISTS BOOK 2

JEN TALTY

Dear Readers,

Welcome to the Special Forces: Operation Alpha Fan-Fiction world!

If you are new to this amazing world, in a nutshell the author wrote a story using one or more of my characters in it. Sometimes that character has a major role in the story, and other times they are only mentioned briefly. This is perfectly legal and allowable because they are going through Aces Press to publish the story.

This book is entirely the work of the author who wrote it. While I might have assisted with brainstorming and other ideas about which of my characters to use, I didn't have any part in the process or writing or editing the story.

I'm proud and excited that so many authors loved my characters enough that they wanted to write them into their own story. Thank you for supporting them, and me!

READ ON!

Xoxo

Susan Stoker

CHAPTER 1

The hot Florida sun beat down on the Inter-coastal Waterway, dancing across the ripples conceived by a warm breeze rolling in off the salty ocean. Hunter Jackson wiped the perspiration beading across his forehead before he pulled back the throttles of his Absolute 50Fly luxury cabin cruiser, though others might consider it a yacht.

Hunter called it home.

There is nothing better than living on the water.

"This has been an amazing day." His buddy, Dude Cooper, a Navy SEAL, stretched out on the seat behind the console. Hunter had first met him when he'd volunteered for a special assignment with the Air Force Fire Protection Specialists in an undisclosed area. Dude was a bomb tech, and while deployed, there had been four bombs set off outside of a small town in the middle of a forest. It took almost two days to control the brush fires.

But the strangest part had been when his current Crew Chief, Ace Enders, who had been on assignment with him, was good friends with one of Dude's team members, Tex Keegan, who had been instrumental in helping Ace nail the bastards that had killed his high school sweetheart and her family.

Hunter glanced over his shoulder. Ace had made himself comfortable on the stern bench, beer in hand. If Hunter ever needed anything, Ace would be at his side with the snap of a finger. Men didn't come any better than him.

Even if Ace had gotten him shot a few months back.

Hunter rubbed his thigh, remembering the bullet tearing through his muscle. If he had to do it all over again, he'd glady take the bullet since it had helped to save Ace's wife and her mother.

They were good people.

"Cheyenne would have loved it here," Dude said.

"It would have been nice to meet her and your daughter." While Hunter meant the words wholeheartedly, he didn't really want it to happen. Not because he didn't care. He didn't begrudge either one of his buddies newfound relationship statuses, but he did miss always being Ace's wingman. Before he got married, Ace had offered himself to every special assignment he could get his hands on with Hunter. When other friends fell in love, changing their lives, Hunter and Ace continued the pack of bachelorhood.

"I'll have to plan a couple of vacation days and bring the family."

"You're welcome anytime." Hunter swallowed, hard. Once upon a time, he'd been madly in love. In fact, he'd been so far under the spell of a woman, he'd planned on getting married and having half a dozen rug rats. But now? The idea of even being around children made his skin prickle with fear. Not to mention, the idea of giving his heart to any woman made him want to rip it from his chest and stomp on it himself.

That would hurt less.

There hadn't been a woman in his life that hadn't hurt him. All starting with his mother. She'd ruined everything in his life and now that she was dying, she wanted to reconcile or some such nonsense.

Well, too late for that, Mom.

Hunter navigated the cruiser through the docks at the marina owned by Ace's mother-in-law. He put one engine in forward, the other in reverse and turned the boat so he could back into his spot.

Ace's wife, Lexi, stood at the end of the dock, waiting for Ace to toss her the stern line. He'd met Lexi shortly after Ace had pulled her from a burning car after witnessing a hit and run accident. It turned out that the same crime family that had killed his teenaged love had set their sights on using the marina to launder money. When Lexi and her mom refused to bring them in as partners, bad things started to happen, but Ace came to the rescue.

Hunter tapped the throttles in gear, then brought them to neutral.

Dude slapped Hunter on the back. "Thanks for this. It's been a long time since I've been able to kick back with the boys."

"My pleasure. Are you sure you don't want to stay for dinner?" Hunter often ended up a third wheel with Ace and Lexi, which hadn't bothered him until recently. Seeing how happy Lexi made Ace, reminded Hunter of things past and for the first time in a long time, he felt a pang of loneliness.

A hint of regret.

A generous dose of resentment.

He'd lived alone since he walked out of his parents's home ten years ago, the summer between his junior and senior year of college. He didn't go back to school, and he hasn't been home since.

Not that he had a house to go home to since his father had sold it when his mother had left him for another man.

And his girlfriend chose her side.

"I appreciate the offer, but I'm going to have to pass," Dude said.

Hunter shut off the engines, snagging the keys and shoving them in the pocket of his jeans. He made his way to the stern of the boat where Ace and Lexi had gathered, arms draped over each other, kissing. They were still in the newlywed stage of their relationship where every chance they got, they were groping each other. Hunter once made a comment it. Ace replied something about making babies.

Well, that wouldn't happen in public, hopefully, so why did they have to touch and kiss all the time? Even when Hunter had been in love, he hadn't participated in random public displays of affection very often.

Okay, well he did more than he wanted to admit.

Or remember.

He didn't want to miss her, even though she haunted his every dream.

"How was it out there today?" Lexi asked, leaning into Ace, her hand resting on his chest.

"Didn't catch much," Ace said, kissing her cheek. "How was your day?"

"Uneventful."

"I hate to break up the party, but I really should run," Dude said.

"We're going to the Waterway for dinner. Would you both like to join us?" Lexi always had a sweet smile and a kind voice. She never left anyone out and always made him feel welcome, even when he was the odd man out.

Hunter could understand how any man would be mesmerized by Lexi's unique look with her tanned complexion, dark, inviting eyes, warm smile, and gentle personality. Deep down, Hunter knew not all women were like his mother.

Or his ex.

"I've got a date with a C-150 at three-thirty in the morning, so I really need to hit the sack soon," Dude said.

"What about you, Hunter? Will you join us?" Lexi asked.

"Thanks, but I'm going to cook up the fish we caught today. Got to eat it while it's fresh."

Lexi pursed her lips, giving him a sad, disappointed look. She didn't feel sorry for him, but she'd once told him she sensed an emptiness in him that could have only been created by heartache. He'd laughed it off, even though he knew Lexi was not only perceptive, but dead-on right.

She was always right.

Hunter glanced toward the shore and his breath hitched, catching the beauty he'd never forgotten. He lowered his sunglasses, peering over the rim. "No fucking way."

A tall, slender woman with long blond hair bouncing over her shoulders like in a shampoo commercial, strolled across the parking lot wearing what could only be described as pink fuck-me pumps and a floral dress that hugged her body like a second skin. She sported big white sunglasses and her plump, glossy lips attracted a ray of sunshine, lighting up her sultry face. She looked like an actress or model promenading across the red carpet.

And reminded him of everything in his past.

And everything he thought his future would hold.

"Whoa. Who is that?" Lexi asked.

"Claire Thompson." The name rolled off his tongue, triggering a kaleidoscope of memories swirling in his mind, sending heat to all the wrong places.

"You know her?" Ace asked.

"Yeah," he said with a dry, scratchy throat.

"And? Who is she to you?" Dude asked.

"My ex-girlfriend or my step-sister, depending on how you want to spin it."

When Claire Thompson had been given Hunter's address, she expected a top-notch yacht club, not your average-joe marina where she had to assume he had the nicest, most expensive boat in all the marina. She paused for a second at the end of the dock, staring at a bare-chested Hunter on the back of what she guessed to be at least a fifty-foot Absolute. Nice boat, but a little small and not quite right for a man that was worth something like forty-two million dollars.

Of course Hunter wanted to pretend he didn't come from money. He'd always had a hard time dealing with the idea he could do whatever he wanted, whenever he wanted, which is why she totally understood his career choice.

Her body shivered, remembering how his fingers

dug into her ass and how his lips sizzled against her skin. Every lover she'd had since Hunter had paled in comparison.

She sucked in a deep breath, the salty air burning her lungs as she stepped with wobbly legs onto the dock. Wearing three-inch heels had been a dumb idea, but Hunter had always loved it when she wore sexy shoes and form-fitting clothes. He worshiped her body and admired her brains.

At one time, he loved her.

And she still loved him.

He lowered his head, looking over his designer sunglasses, mouth gaping open.

At least she still had an effect on him ten years later. Though she wasn't exactly sure if he was gawking or glaring. Either way, she figured he wouldn't be too happy she'd just shown up. The last time she'd seen him, he'd mentioned that living in a dumpster would be better than ever having to lay eyes on her again.

The closer she got to the boat, the slower she walked. Hunter and his friends just stood on the stern, staring at her. She breathed slowly, trying to calm her racing pulse. Clutching her purse, she hoped her trembling hands didn't give away her lack of confidence. She hated being vulnerable, but she'd made a promise.

If anything, she was as good as her word.

"Hello, Hunter," she said, lifting her sunglasses up, letting them rest on the top of her head, keeping her recently- styled hair from falling in her face.

"What are you doing here?" He planted his hands on his hips, just over his low-hanging shorts. He'd gotten a tattoo of some kind of compass with fire around it on his chest.

She tilted her head, searching the side of his arm for the tattoo he'd gotten when they'd been dating. He must have sensed what she was searching for as he twisted his body, giving her a birds-eye view of the two hearts she'd doodled on her notebooks in high school with the words: *2 hearts 1 love.*

Heat burned her cheeks.

"I've come to talk some sense into you."

"You came on your own? Or did someone send you?" His accusatory tone smacked her skin like large water pellets slamming to the ground.

"Does it matter?"

"It always matters." Hunter stepped back, ducking his head into a cooler. He lifted a beer, twisting the top and chugging half.

"You're not going to invite me aboard or introduce me to your friends?" She put one hand on her hip.

"Nope. And I'm not going home either, so you can tell my mother I got the message."

"You're being a childish asshole."

"I'm sorry. As much as I'd like to stick around and see how this show ends, I've got to go," one of the men said as he hopped off the boat.

"We should go too," the woman said.

The man with her helped her off the boat, and the trio headed toward the parking lot, glancing over their shoulders a few times.

Claire took a deep calming breath. "Help me on the boat," she said.

"Not with those shoes on. You'll either tear the leather seats or break your neck."

"Fine," she said, leaning over, pulling one shoe off, then the other. Tucking her purse under her armpit, she dangled the shoes from one hand, holding out the other.

"I still don't want you on my boat." He took a long draw from his beer, eyeing her with his golden eyes. "Go home, Claire. Tell my mother whatever you want, but I'm not rushing to her bedside."

"Your mother didn't send me." She tossed her

shoes and purse on the boat before grabbing the railing and climbing aboard. "Your father did."

He gagged on his beer, spewing the liquid onto the deck.

She breezed past him, lifting the lid on the outside cooler and grabbing a cold one for herself. Her entire life, she'd been called a contradiction. Raised a socialite, she had a flare for the finer things in life, like her three-hundred-dollar shoes that lay on the back bench of the luxury cruiser. Her closet was filled with designer clothes, much like the one-of-a-kind dress she had on which was created by an up-and-coming designer.

Claire might have been homecoming queen and dabbled in modeling during high school, but she'd also been captain of her volleyball team, which got her a college scholarship to the same school Hunter had been recruited to play golf. She'd never been afraid of hard work and upon graduating, a year after Hunter had walked out of her life, she volunteered for the Peace Corps, spending over three years as a health advisor in a remote village in South America. She had survived living on about a dollar a day, with no running water, and no air-conditioning. Her bathroom was a shared outhouse, and she had to take bucket baths.

She continued to work for the Peace Corps in the recruitment office as well as occasionally taking short assignments when needed.

Holding out the beer, she waited for Hunter to take it and be the gentleman she knew he could be. But when he just stared at her, she shrugged her shoulders and twisted off the top with ease. She'd developed a taste for beer in college and it had never left her, but it always reminded her of the only man she would ever love.

"My father asked you to come? Why would he do that?"

"Because he's not a selfish prick, like his son."

"Swearing isn't becoming of a lady." Hunter snagged another beer before plopping himself down on the back bench.

She laughed. "I'm not a docile little lady, and you used to think it was cute when I uttered the unexpected obscenity."

"I'd be lying if you weren't still, well… drop-dead gorgeous, but that doesn't change the past." He stretched his legs out, resting his feet on the cushion. "I'll call my dad later and tell him you came, asked me to come home, and that I said no."

"What is wrong with you?" She sat down on the chair across from him. The cruiser was more of a home than a boat, so it wasn't surprising that Hunter had opted to live on it. He had always had a thing for the water. "Your mother is dying, and all she wants is to see her youngest before she goes. Your sister misses you. Your brother is a dad now and would love to have you meet your nephew. I don't think that is too much to ask for you to return, just to give a dying woman some peace, regardless of the past."

"You called me selfish, well, I must get that from my mother since all she thinks about is herself." He didn't look in her direction, keeping his head turned, facing the Intercoastal. He waved to a boat that eased by.

"I didn't expect you to come home three years ago when my dad passed away unexpectedly, but Louisa is your mother, and she's been heartbroken ever since you left."

Hunter laughed. "So heartbroken she couldn't tear herself away from her lover to save her family." Every syllable was laced with the same angry tone he had the day he'd found out about the affair.

"My parents were separated, and you chose to ignore the fact that your parents fought all the time and barely shared the same bed anymore."

He snapped his attention to her, ripping off his sunglasses. "You didn't come home and find your mother sucking face with the man you expected to be your father-in-law, not your step-father."

"I can't believe we're having this same argument. What's worse is that you've held on to this all these years. Your father and siblings have forgiven her. They are at your mother's bedside every day. Your father, and even his wife, Judy, were there for your mother when my dad died. If you had stuck around long enough to work through what happened, you'd see how much better off everyone was."

"That's fucked up," he said, dropping his feet to the floor and leaning forward. "My mother didn't come to my matches because she was too busy screwing your dad. Your dad didn't go to your games because he was holed up in some hotel with my mother. Have you forgotten those betrayals? Forgotten that their affair had been going on for years?" He stood and closed the gap, lifting her out of her chair, holding her gaze with fire in his honey eyes. "In the last ten years, I've heard from my mother only a handful of times, and each time all she'd cared about was explaining why it happened and how happy she'd finally been with your dad. She didn't once care about me or how I felt. Only that I'd accept what she'd done and act as if it were the best thing since sliced bread."

She swallowed. His fingers curled around her arms, burning their imprint into her skin like a cattle prod. They'd all been angry and upset when the truth came out. Claire had told her father that she hated him. She'd cried for hours, feeling humiliated. But the worst part was that her boyfriend couldn't, or wouldn't, give her any comfort.

He tilted his head, leaning in, a scant few inches from her face. Licking his lips, he moved in for the kill, pressing his warm lips over hers, teasing her with his tongue.

Her body stiffened for a moment, before turning into putty. Her chest rose, compressing her breasts against his hard body. Ten years ago, he'd been her world. Her rock. The only person who truly understood her. She wrapped her arms around his broad shoulders.

He snapped his head back, breaking off the tumultuous kiss. "My mother made her choice, and it wasn't her family."

"And you made yours, and it wasn't me."

He cocked his head, dropping his hands to his sides. "That's rich. I begged you to come with me."

"You ordered me, demanded I give up my education, and never speak to my family again. I loved you, but I loved my family too. My sisters and brothers needed me. My mother needed me, and I needed you, but you…" She poked his chest. "…acted like a spoiled brat, and when things didn't go your way, took off." Her insides still shook from the earth-shattering kiss. Memories of their love affair collided with the pain he'd caused his entire family when he'd cut off all communication, blocking phone numbers, going dark on the internet, making himself a ghost.

But mostly, how he'd punctured her heart, leaving it with a gaping hole that no matter what she tried, she'd never be able to fill the space he left behind.

His eyes narrowed to tiny slits. "Joining the Air Force and becoming a Fire Protection Specialist was the best thing that ever happened to me. I have no regrets."

"Neither do I." She swallowed the guttural sob that lodged in her throat.

"Good. Now get off my boat and go home."

She folded her arms, sitting back down. "I'm not going anywhere until you agree to come back with me."

"When hell freezes over," he said.

Dark clouds rolled in off the ocean. The smell of salty rain filled the humid air that clung to her skin.

"I can wait," she said defiantly.

"Suit yourself." He stepped into the galley, closing the door.

She heard the click of the lock.

It was going to be a long night.

CHAPTER 2

The wind howled as it brought the first few raindrops that pelted the fiberglass boat. It never rained long in Florida during the summer months, but when it did, it came down hard, fast, and with loud claps of thunder. The cruiser rocked with the waves of the Intercoastal Waterways.

Hunter lay on the king-size bed that took up most of the single bedroom, staring up at the portal on the bow of the boat. His stomach growled, but he didn't feel like getting out of bed. It had been over an hour since he'd left Claire sitting on the deck. He assumed she was long gone by now, considering the storm that was coming. He ran his fingers across his lips. Kissing her had been stupid, and he had no idea why he'd done it other than he wanted to know if she still tasted like honey.

Which she did.

He blinked his eyes, pulling up an image of his mother when he'd been a small boy. Her dark hair touching her shoulders. He had his mother's whiskey-colored eyes. When he was a kid, he thought his mother was the most beautiful woman ever, always full of life. He couldn't imagine what battling stage-four ovarian cancer was doing to her body.

The evening sky lit up with multiple lightning strikes. Thunder pounded as the rain came down in a continuous stream.

"Hunter! Let me in, please."

He sprung from the bed, racing from the room, through the main cabin, eating area, and the galley, finally reaching the door. He unlocked the latch. "What the hell are you still doing here?" He stepped back, helping a drenched Claire down the steps.

"Waiting for hell to freeze over."

"Didn't you see the storm coming?"

She nodded. "I thought you'd let me in when it started to rain."

"I thought you'd leave." He held up his hand. "Stay there, I'll get you a towel."

He left her standing at the threshold, looking like a drowned rat. He should have known. The woman almost never took no for an answer. She had to be one of the most stubborn, pig-headed women he'd ever met. Glancing out the window, he searched for a break in the clouds, but all he found was more darkness.

After getting a towel, he ducked into his room and snagged a pair of shorts and a T-shirt. She'd swim in them, but it was better than the wet dress she currently had on.

"You can change into these." He tossed her the towel and the clothes, making sure he kept a safe distance. His heart pounded against his chest, reminding him of how she'd destroyed it.

"Thank you," she said, ruffling her tangled blond locks with the towel as she breezed by, leaving a scented trail of honey and fresh pineapple. She'd been the hottest girl in high school, and the most popular, and it wasn't because she was rich.

It was because she was as sweet as home-baked cookies and had a big heart. He'd known her his entire life, having grown up at the same country club. As children, they took swimming lessons and played paddle tennis against one another. For the majority of their lives, they'd been friends. Not close friends, since they didn't really hang out together outside of the club, but close enough.

His stomach rumbled. "Claire, have you eaten dinner?" he yelled toward the bedroom.

"No, but don't go to any trouble."

"I won't. But I have to eat." He told himself he'd feed her while they waited for the storm to pass, and then he'd send her packing. He'd just have to make her understand there was nothing left for him at home.

He pulled out all the ingredients he needed to make a pan-seared sea bass with asparagus, which she hated and that made him smile. God, he was an asshole. He took the knife and started chopping the garlic when she stepped in the galley wearing his T-shirt and shorts. They hid her perfect body with their bagginess, but she was still the sexiest woman on the planet.

Razor-sharp pain tinged his finger.

"Fuck," he muttered, dropping the knife. He stared at his hand. A few drops of blood trickled from his index finger.

"Let me do that. You always put too much garlic in anyway." She moved him to the side with her warm, sexy hands. Memories of them roaming his body pelted his brain.

He should have been a real prick and not let her in. He cleaned up his wound, put a Band-Aid on it, and went about heating up the skillet.

She stood next to him, slicing and dicing before reaching across him and dumping the onions, garlic, and other seasonings in the pan with a dash of olive oil. Her hair brushed his shoulder. In college, when they had lived together, they enjoyed cooking together. They moved in the kitchen much like synchronized swimmers cutting through the water with precision.

"I'll finish up. Why don't you go sit down at the table?" He needed to put some distance between their bodies and clear the teenage hormones from his mind. Over the years, he'd run through various potential conversations he might have with her, and none of them included cooking fish together.

"Do you have any white wine?"

"There's a bottle open in the fridge and more in the cooler." Wine was a mistake and he knew it, but he decided to check his prick personality at the door and enjoy a good meal. "Glasses are in that cabinet to the right of the sink."

A loud clap of thunder boomed through the night as more lightning brightened the inside of the boat.

"I love a good thunderstorm," she said, placing a wine glass down next to the stove.

He ignored the tightening in his muscles and the tingling sensation crawling across his fingertips, itching to dig into her soft curves. The fish sizzled as he flipped it. He focused on his growling stomach and sipped his wine, not wanting to go sit at the table and continue to pretend this wasn't the most awkward situation either one of them had ever been in.

"My father really asked you to come?"

"He said you hadn't returned his phone calls, except for a few random text messages that work was too hectic for you to get away."

He placed a plate of food in front of her and joined her at the table.

"Imagine my surprise when I get here and find out you're on a week's vacation." She looked to the ceiling, pressing her forefinger to her temple. "And today was the first day."

"Spying on me?"

She shook her head, letting out a sarcastic laugh. "I called the base when I landed. It took being transferred to a few different people before I was informed you'd be gone for the week."

"You're lucky I'm still here. But you still wasted

your time."

"I had to try," she said, lowering her gaze. "You're mom is in bad shape."

"My dad texted me yesterday and said Mom had maybe a month left and that at this point, she refused all treatment except for pain medication." He gulped his wine. He'd actually bought a plane ticket to go back to Kent Island, Maryland, leaving tomorrow morning at seven, but he'd decided not to go. It wasn't just that he had struggled to forgive his mother, or that he'd become estranged with his siblings and father, but there were certain things he just couldn't get out of his mind.

No one could deny how much he'd been hurt, or what it had done to see his mother adjusting her clothing as she and Mr. Thompson stepped from the master bedroom. Hunter might have been an adult, but that would fuck up any young man.

"It's not just your mom who wants to see you."

Hunter picked at the food on his plate. The first few years after he'd left home had been fueled by anger. He dealt with it by becoming the best Fire Protection Specialist and ignored his past, including his money, but then he wanted this boat, so he tapped into his trust fund and that's what triggered an onslaught of messages from his father.

His sister, Emily, had sent him a nasty-gram a few years ago, telling him to get his head out of his ass. His brother constantly sent him pictures of family gatherings. He knew more about them than they did about him.

Not that there was anything to know. He worked. He fished. He worked.

"I don't know about that. What little correspondence I've had with Emily and Miles has been tainted with resentment." A sentiment he understood and had held onto for years. They hadn't been the one to catch their mother, nor the one who had to break the news to their father, but they both seemed to blame Hunter. Not for the break-up of their parents' marriage, but for hurting their mother.

He chugged his wine before pouring another hearty glass.

"I'd go easy on that."

"I'd mind your own business," he said, wishing he could take back the harsh tone.

She leaned back, folding her arms under her breasts.

This is so not the right time to consider her naked body under his T-shirt, though it was a very nice distraction from pondering if he should grant his mother her dying wish, or hold onto anger for the rest of his life. He'd wrapped himself in a bubble of resentment, which protected his heart, but walled him off from having any meaningful relationships, even with his brothers-in-arms.

He swallowed that revelation.

"You're a piece of work," she said, shaking her head. "All you have to do is show up, say hello, and then you can go back to hiding out on your boat, pretending you have a life, when really, all you have is a lot of nothing."

"You know jack shit about my life," he said with a snarl. "I have a great career and fantastic friends. Friends that won't fuck me over like my own family. Or my girlfriend."

"Seriously? You're going to sit there and tell me I screwed you over? Do you hear yourself? You're so god damned angry over something that happened ten years ago. You've never moved past. No. You've chose to make it the bane of your existence."

He opened his mouth, but she cocked her head and arched a brow, so he snapped his mouth shut. For years, he believed it would simply take time to get past what had happened.

And to get over Claire.

Only neither of those things happened.

"All right, you win. I'll go home."

Claire fluffed the pillow Hunter had given her and tried to get comfortable on the sofa. Why she'd insisted on taking the couch when he'd offered her a nice, plush, king-size bed, she had no idea, other than she was brutally stubborn.

A trait that got her in trouble.

Often.

The first year he'd been gone, she tracked his whereabouts and half a dozen times, she booked airline tickets to go see him. But every time she got to the airport, her stubbornness prevented her from taking the trip. She cringed, remembering the amount of money she'd spent that year all because she thought HE should be the one to come to her since he's the one who called things off.

She pulled the soft, 600-thread-count sheets to her chin. The wind and rain had died down, but the boat rocked gently in the water. She'd had a crush on Hunter since she could remember. At school, he barely gave her the time of day, but at the club, she had his full attention, except for when he was on the golf course. The first time he'd made the cut for the club championship, at the ripe old age of sixteen, she'd offered to be his caddy. The only time she ever golfed had been with him. He'd always told her she should take up the game, but it was only fun if she played with him.

It wasn't until after he'd won the club championship that year that she told him she liked him as more than a friend.

She smiled, remembering the stunned look on his face after she'd kissed him. He'd blinked a half-dozen times and opened and closed his mouth a dozen more until he wrapped his arms around her and bruised her lips with a burning kiss.

Those days were long gone, and they were both very different people.

The light from his room seeped out into the main cabin. "This is ridiculous. That sofa is the most uncomfortable thing in the world. The only thing about this boat that sucks."

"I'm not going to ask you to give up your bed. Besides, I lived in a third-world country for three years on a foam bed topper. This is like the Ritz, comparatively."

"You did what?" He stepped into the room wearing nothing but boxers and muscles.

"You didn't know I was in the Peace Corps after college?"

"No, but I was either in basic training, fire school, or deployed for the first four years after I left. I did hear you worked for the Peace Corps, though. I just figured it was in the office. You were always good at managing things that helped people." He scratched the back of his head.

"How on earth did you know I worked for the Peace Corps, but not know I was a volunteer and lived in South America for three years."

"In one of my sister's random emails where she barraters me for not coming home mentioned something about your career."

Wow. He'd really gotten over her.

Quickly.

Of course, she dealt with her grief over their break-up by disconnecting as much as possible.

But it hadn't helped to erase the love she still felt for him.

"Come on." Standing at the side of the sofa, he held out a hand.

"I'm not kicking you out of your room."

"It's a king-size bed. We've slept in smaller."

She raised a brow as her heart hammered in her chest. "I'm not going to sleep with you."

"Yeah, you are. And the key word is sleep. Not sex. We used to sleep in that double bed we had all the time and not have sex."

"We'd wake up and have sex."

"That's true." He leaned over, taking her by the hand. "But I won't be able to sleep knowing you're out here on this. I can promise I won't even think about it, much less touch you."

"That's exactly what every woman wants to hear when a man is wooing her to bed." She stood, sliding her hands from his, snagging the pillow.

He raised his arms. "I'm trying to be nice and respectful here, but I also want to make sure we both get some sleep."

"I get the right side," she said. Good grief, what the hell was she doing agreeing to share his bed? Did she have some sadomasochistic tendencies she didn't know about?

Or had she just lost her mind?

"You're still particular about that?"

"Aren't you?" She held the hem of his shirt down, making sure it covered her ass. She should have kept his shorts on.

"About what side I sleep on? God, no. Then again, I generally don't have women in my bed."

She stopped at the doorway.

"Umph." He bumped into her.

"Generally? What does that mean?"

He pressed his hand into the small of her back, nudging her forward. "It means I'm not seeing anyone and haven't in a while and don't like women on my boat. Cramps my style."

That statement sent her insides on a roller-coaster ride. The downhill turns were filled with jealousy over any woman who'd had him after her. The uphill twists were all about the fact he hadn't been with anyone in a while.

The only question was: what constituted awhile and did he stay at their places instead?

She mentally smacked herself as she pulled back the sheets and slipped onto the soft, but firm mattress.

The bed shifted as he sat down, his back to her. The pitter-patter of light rain drops echoed off the boat. As he twisted, the outside light gleamed through the porthole like a ray of sunshine on the heart tattoo. Without thinking, she reached out and traced the letters inside the heart. "I can't believe you didn't change this."

He rolled to his side, propping himself on his elbow. "I honestly never thought to change it. Besides, I like it."

"Your father was so pissed when you got that." Mindlessly, she continued to run her fingers on his shoulders.

"I remember being upset with you for not getting a matching one."

"Back then, it scared me too much."

"Does that mean you have one now?"

"I've got a couple of them," she admitted, jerking her hand away. "We should get some sleep." As if she could relax enough to doze even for a short period of time. As soon as he drifted off, she planned on sneaking out, which was stupid. She didn't have to stay in his bed, and she certainly didn't care if he thought her rude for not taking him up on his sort of chivalrous act.

"Where?" he asked, rolling to his back.

"Back of my neck and lower back."

"Of what?"

She tucked her hands under her cheek and closed her eyes. "On my lower back is a set of butterflies." Taking in a deep calming breath, she searched for the courage to tell him.

"You always did love those insects." His chest rose and fell in a rhythmic pattern. "And the other one?"

"The same one you have on your biceps."

CHAPTER 3

"Are you serious?" Hunter bolted upright, ripping the covers from their bodies. He reached across her and flicked on the reading lamp. "You've got this on your neck?" He tapped the tattoo he'd gotten right before they graduated from high school. The intention had been that they would both get the tattoo, but after watching the needles dig into his arm, Claire had chickened out. He couldn't blame her. It did hurt, and the smell of burning flesh was an acquired taste. "When?"

"About seven years ago." She sat up and rubbed the back of her neck, her hair flowing over her shoulders. "I'd finished my initial service for the Peace Corps and extended my stay. I went home for a week for a family wedding, and I found of box of stuff from high school. The drawing we took to the guy who did yours was there, and I remembered the promise I made. So, I got it."

He opted to ignore the fact that the wedding she referred to had been his mother to her father. A thought that still weirded him out on so many levels. "Can I see it?" His pulse raced faster than the first time he'd run into a burning building. Of course, the second he'd crossed the threshold, he didn't notice his heartbeat and his training kicked in.

No one had ever trained him on how to deal with an ex-girlfriend who fulfilled a promise long after the relationship ended, never telling him about it either.

She turned, raising her hair up, exposing the back of her neck and a matching tattoo.

"Why? Why did you do that?" He reached out with a shaky hand, his index finger hovering over the letters. He recoiled when she let her hair fall. The wavy locks bounced over her shoulders.

"I don't know. Maybe in a weird way, I thought I owed it to you. Or maybe it was closure."

He pushed her hair to the side, unmasking the symbol that once represented their undying love. He inched closer, studying the design. "This is a little different than mine."

"No, it's not." She tried to turn, but he grabbed her arms, holding her steady.

"What's this?" He followed the lines—there were letters etched in the lining of one of the hearts—H K J. "My initials?" His throat dropped to his stomach. A woman didn't permanently scar her skin with a man's name when she was looking for closure.

She cleared her throat, smoothing down her hair as she scooted to the edge of the bed. "I was feeling sentimental."

"Seriously? You tattooed my initials into your neck over an emotional moment about the past?"

She sprung from the bed, her head hitting the low ceiling.

"Shit," she whispered, sitting back down.

"Are you okay?" He palmed her shoulder, his fingers tangling in her soft hair.

"My head is fine, but I'm not." She shrugged his arm off. "It wasn't an emotional moment, as you called it. You're a huge part of my past and I wanted something from that time. My dad and your mom had just gotten married and—"

"And their union made you want to engrave me on your neck?"

"I'm sorry this is freaking you out."

"I'm not the one that just leapt from the bed." He

patted the mattress. “I am however, very curious.” He was more than curious. He was utterly fascinated, not to mention it inflated his bruised ego when it came to how easily Claire let him walk away.

“I never had any intention of telling you.” She pulled her hair to the side, twirling it in her hands as she leaned back against the headboard. “I thought if I got the tattoo I would be able to prove to myself that I was finally over you leaving me. The initials I had done a year later when I got the butterflies.”

“So, I was an afterthought,” he mumbled, unsure of the sensations swirling in his gut. He positioned himself next to her, their arms touching ever so slightly, but enough that it generated the kind of raw heat that reminded him she was every bit a woman.

“I wouldn’t say an afterthought, exactly. I really don’t know how to explain it all without sounding like a crazy, psycho ex-girlfriend.”

“Yeah, it’s a little nuts.”

“Trust me, I know. But getting over you dumping me was the hardest thing I’ve ever had to do.”

“Harder than living in a third-world country?” he asked.

“At least you can admit you’re the one who broke up with me.”

“We both called it quits.” Everything that she’d

ever meant to him came crashing down on his heart, squeezing the life out of him. He'd been telling himself for years that he didn't need her or even want her. But the ugly truth was he'd never gotten over the fact that she'd never chased after him. Never called him or looked for him. A childish thing to hold on to, but it still hurt as much as how his mother scolded him for telling his father what he'd seen before she got a chance to do it herself. His mother made it clear it was her life, and he had no right butting in.

Only it affected everything he'd done from that day forward.

Now, to find out, Claire had done the one thing she couldn't do when they were together, years after they broke up, he didn't know what to think about his inability to call her over the years. Not once did he ever think that she, or his mother for that matter, was hurting like he had been.

"We didn't fight for each other," she said. Her dark blue eyes captured his gaze, holding him hostage.

"You told me if I left, we were done."

"Only after you said if I loved you I'd drop out of college and run off with you, turning my back on my family."

He lay down, resting his head on her thighs, looking up at her. "You were always a stubborn mule."

"I still am," she said, smiling, running her fingers through his hair. "But so were you."

"Tell me something. Did you wear those heels and dress to get me all hot and bothered so you could get me to do what you wanted?"

"What do you think?"

"You could make a pair of sneakers look sexy." He reached up, cupping the back of her neck, rolling his thumb in a tiny circle just behind her earlobe, drawing her plump, luscious lips closer to his.

"What are you doing?"

"I'm getting ready to kiss you."

"You promised you'd keep your hands to yourself." Her pink tongue darted out, rolling across her mouth in an exotic ritual.

He lifted his head, getting lost in her sea-blue eyes. "I can roll over right now and go to sleep, or I can do something as crazy as tattooing your initials on my arm."

Her hot breath covered his face in a warm blanket. "Us being together isn't a good idea."

"I know. But it seems like we both need something so we can move forward."

She arched a brow. "Are you suggesting we have one last romp in the sack as a way to get some sort of resolution to the way we ended things ten years ago?"

"Either that, or I could go get C A T tattooed in my hearts."

"You know how I feel about my initials. My parents didn't think that one through."

"But I love pussy...cats," he said, enjoying how easily they fell into their old banter, like the ten years was more like ten days.

"Not a good line to get me in bed."

"We're already there, so how about we stop talking." He took her mouth in a tender, deep, passionate kiss, probing every succulent crevice.

Her hands glided across his chest as she sprawled out next to him. Their lovemaking had always been filled with a combination of delicate compassion and a raw craving that left them breathless. Not a single woman since had satisfied his appetite the way she had. Sure, he'd had some great sex with some really hot women, but they didn't make his blood turn to smoldering lava.

His hands roamed her body, feeling every soft curve. All he wanted was to feel her warm skin against his. Lifting her shirt up, he ducked his head into the crevice of her neck, kissing and nibbling on her earlobe. He palmed her breast enjoying her soft moans.

His body told him to devour every inch of her.

His brain whispered to stop.

His heart begged him to stand up and go sleep on the extremely uncomfortable sofa.

He jerked his head back, staring down at her.

"What's wrong?" she asked.

"Nothing." He cupped her chin with his thumb and forefinger, ignoring his heart. She couldn't hurt him anymore. They weren't destined to be together, and after this trip home to give closure to his mother, Claire would walk out of his life again.

No. He'd walk out of hers.

Slipping his hand into her cotton panties, he cupped her smooth, bare sex, circling his fingers over her hard nub.

She arched her back, raising her breasts to his mouth. Her hips rolled slowly against his palm. He remembered every inch of her body and knew exactly what it craved. He teased her, nibbling on her nipples, slowly sliding his finger in and out. She tried to get him to increase the speed and pressure, but he kept his strokes deliberate and soft.

Teasing her to the brink of begging had always

been a pleasure he'd never quite been able to capture again.

In one swift motion, he yanked her underwear to her ankles, tossing them across the room. He stared at her shaven womanhood that glistened with desire. Cupping both her breasts, he bent over, first breathing on her before licking gently.

She clutched his head, pushing him against her.

"Please, don't torture me. I can't take it."

"But it's half the fun." He pulled back just enough to continue brushing his lips and tongue gently across her soft sex. She smelled like bottled sunshine and tasted like a warm day on the beach with a tinge of salt in the air.

Her fingers dug into his scalp as she arched her back, raising her hips higher.

He pinched and twisted her nipples, enjoying her deep throaty groans.

"Jesus, would you just do it," she said in a pant.

He smiled against her, clamping his mouth over her, sucking on her hard nub until she dug her ankles into his back. Her body jerking and thrashing about the bed, legs squeezing his head and her creamy climax spilled out, coating his mouth and fingers, igniting a deep burn across his skin.

He had to have her. Right now. He couldn't wait.

He kissed the inside of her thigh, making his way down her long silky legs. Standing, he removed his shorts and found a condom. He held the foil wrapper up to his mouth, preparing to tear it with his teeth.

She'd propped up on her elbows, knees bent, staring at him with a mischievous smile. "You know what I want now."

"Seriously? You still have to do that? Every time you have sex?"

She cocked her head. "Don't all women?"

He wished. "Not the ones I've met."

"Well, sex shouldn't happen without it."

He tossed the condom on the bed. "Do with me what you want. I'm not going to complain."

"Never complain, only beg me to stop."

"Yeah, in about three seconds, unless you want this to end with oral."

"That would be a travesty," she whispered.

He sucked in a breath, gritting his teeth as she took him in her soft hands, gliding them up and down. Her tongue swirling over the top, taking just the tip into her mouth.

He hissed as she squeezed his shaft, cupping him, easing him into her mouth with her hot lips. He used to tease her about her insatiable appetite for giving blowjobs. The first one she'd ever given, he swore she had to be lying that she'd never done it before. The way she admired him as she toyed with him, bringing him the kind of pleasure that made a man weak at his knees.

He let out a long guttural groan, clenching his fists, doing his best not to grab her head and slam deep inside her mouth. Though, he knew from past experience, she wouldn't be opposed, but that is not how he wanted this to end.

"You've got to stop," he ground out, swelling inside her, on the verge of losing all control.

She reached for the condom, tearing it open with her teeth.

"Christ, that is so hot," he said.

She smiled, rolling the barrier over the length of him. "So, your favorite, or mine."

"Yours." He might last a little longer that way, saving himself some embarrassment of acting like a horney teenager who climaxed the second he was touched.

She raised up on her knees, wrapping her arms around his shoulders, pressing her lips against his. "Get on your back, Hunter," she whispered. She'd never been afraid to express herself or ask for what she wanted, needed.

Who was he to deny her?

She straddled him, resting her sex against his. She rubbed her clit gently over him while she plucked at her nipples, biting her lower lip. Gliding one hand down her stomach, she flicked her fingers across herself, scraping her nails against his sensitive skin.

He grabbed her hips, moving them back and forth slightly, creating more friction where she needed it most. Biting down on the inside of his mouth, he held onto her so tight he worried he bruised her delicate skin. Her moans grew louder, and her movements harder and faster until she raised up slightly, taking him inside.

He thrust his hips up, holding her over him for a long moment, before repeating the motion. She tightened around him. "Yes," she said in a long moan, drenching him with her hot climax. She dropped her hands to his chest, her hair spilling over his face and body. "Hunter," she whispered, grinding as he thrust inside her. He grunted as he flipped her on her back, ramming himself deep inside, burying his face in her neck as his body rippled with the kind of pleasure only she could give him.

He jerked, and his stomach twitched as he

collapsed on top of her. Their chests heaving up and down, breathless. He kissed her neck and earlobe.

Making love to her again didn't bring him closure. It only reminded him of all the reasons why he loved her in the first place. It rattled his mind and opened the burning hole in his heart.

CHAPTER 4

Hunter slipped from the bed, careful not to wake sleeping beauty.

Quietly, he closed the bedroom door and made his way to the back deck of the yacht. The morning only tinged with the promise of the warm sun.

He glanced over his shoulder as if he could see Claire tucked away in his bed.

He'd opened Pandora's box and he didn't think he'd ever be able to close it again. The second he fought his first fire, he knew that's what he'd been born to do

Just like loving Claire.

He couldn't deny his feelings any more than he could ignore the guilt he tried to bury in some dark corner of his heart.

Deep down, he knew he'd return home to say good-bye to his mother. He had to and not just for her, but for him as well.

"Look Daddy, it's uncle Hunter!" Elle Stavros waved from the edge of the dock.

Jaxson, a senior firefighter, and a single father, made his way toward Hunter, holding his daughter's hand.

"Shhh, quite. People are still sleeping," Jax said.

"Hey squirt. What are you two doing here so early?" Hunter asked.

"Uncle Ace said we could take his boat out and go fishing."

"Oh, pretty shoes." Elle pointed to the pair of pink heels that Claire had kicked off. "Do you have a girlfriend now? Does she have a friend she can introduce to my dad? Eh needs a girlfriend bad."

Hunter covered his mouth, biting back his laughter.

"Elle, why don't you go start prepping the boat. I'll be right along." Jax jumped aboard while Elle skipped down the dock, swinging her arms back and forth.

"Out of the mouths of babes."

"Yeah, but now I'm going to be fielding a million questions about what happened to the lady with the pink shoes." Jax shook his head. "Not to mention Elle just tried to fix me up with the school nurse."

"Oh, my, God. That's classic," Hunter said. He'd always enjoyed Elle and her spitfire personality and he respected Jax for his ability to raise a child all by himself since Elle's mother had died shortly after Elle had been born.

"Ace told me you got a visit from some hot chick, but he said something about her being your step-sister."

"Technically, she is. But she was my girlfriend before my mom married her dad."

"That's just weird and please don't ever tell that to Elle. I would have no idea how to explain that one and Elle has been asking so many questions lately about boys and girls and shit I'm not ready to discuss."

"That little girl is going to grow up on you." Hunter slapped his buddy on the shoulder. "But not to worry. She won't cross Claire's path. I'm flying home with her today to see my mom. She doesn't have much time left." Hunter's throat was thick with emotion. The realization he would be coming face to face with his family under such intense circumstances sent his mind in a million directions.

"Wait. Claire as in the one who created the tatt on your shoulder? The girlfriend that—"

"Yep. That one." Hunter didn't need to hear is buddy rattle off what little he'd shared about his life one night when he'd had a little too much to drink.

"And she spent the night?" Jax pointed to the cabin. "In there. With you?"

Hunter wasn't the type to kiss and tell, but when he kept his mouth closed, well he figured that spoke volumes.

Jax took a seat on the back bench. "You okay?"

Hunter nodded, leaning against the consul. "But I'll be honest, going home is freaking me right the fuck out. I've seen my father maybe five times in the last ten years. My brother about the same. My sister only twice and mom, well, not at all."

"I can't imagine going longer than a month without seeing my mom." Jax waved his hand toward Ace's boat where Elle was taking out all the fishing gear. "But all Elle has are a few pictures. She had only hours with her mother and she doesn't remember a thing about her. Only what I tell her and since I barely knew her mother, that's not much."

"She's turning out just fine."

Jax let out a long breath. "That's not the point.

You've seen how she is with Lexi and even my nanny Mauve. She's starved for female affection. I could be the best dad in all the land, but nothing can ever replace ones mother."

"You are the best dad and my situation is so very different. My mother had a choice and she chose to break up the family for her own selfish reasons."

"So, you choose to continue the madness and punish her. That my friend, is damned selfish."

"Oh, what do you know," Hunter said, waving his hand. "And it doesn't matter. I'm going to fulfill my mother's dying wish and go see her."

Jax leaned forward, resting his forearms on his knees. "Make peace with her. If you don't, you're going to regret it."

Claire smoothed down the front of her dress and sucked in a deep breath. She should have thought about what the morning after would have been like, especially when she woke up, alone, in HIS bed.

"Are you ready?" he called from the deck, his suitcase in hand. "The traffic on ninety-five is going to be a bitch."

She took the hand he offered, climbing the steps

in the same dress she'd shown up in. All she could hope for was that none of his friends would bear witness to her walk of shame. She chomped down on her lower lip. Since when did she care what anyone but her family thought?

"Mind if I drive your rental?" he asked.

"That depends." She slipped her feet into her pumps and followed him down the dock. The night sky was slowly being replaced with the glow of the sun as a few pelicans made their perch for the day on the tall dock posts. "Do you still drive like an old lady?" she asked, trying to ease the tension.

"I never drove slow, but you had a tendency to drive like you were a racecar driver. Not to mention, you were the queen of tailgating."

She snagged the keys to the mid-size sedan from her purse, tossing them to him. "I hate Florida drivers, so you can drive."

Slipping in the back seat, she zipped open her overnight bag.

"What are you doing?"

"Changing my clothes," she said, pulling out her jeans and designer blouse, along with her fancy sneakers. "Keep your eyes up front."

He laughed, glancing in the rearview mirror as he pushed the shifter into reverse.

"I'm serious." She reached around her back, pulling down her zipper. Holding up her shirt, she slipped her arms out of her dress. As soon as he focused on the road in front of them, she shimmied out of her dress, pulling her top over her head, and hiking up her jeans. She found her make-up case and climbed over the seat just as he pulled out onto the highway. "Did I tell you we've got your father's jet?"

"You neglected to tell me that little piece of information." He handed her his phone. "Mind canceling my flight?"

"Why bother? You're going to lose your money anyway."

"Not on Southwest."

She snapped her head in his direction. "Since when do you fly a discounted airline?"

"Since I don't live off my father's money."

She laughed. "Because you can afford an Absolute luxury yacht on your salary. Not to mention I saw a Harley Davidson Ultra Limited in the parking lot and a Roadster, which were both your dream vehicles."

He shook his head. "All right. I've used some of my trust, but I don't live off it. I pay my own bills."

"I'm just teasing you. I might have roughed it for

a few years, but that didn't stop Mommy and Daddy from sending me care packages with all sorts of goodies, including a fancy coffee machine that I couldn't use and donated to the local hospital."

"You've always been a bit of a do-gooder."

"I still am, but I will admit to being spoiled, and I do enjoy flying first class."

"When you're used to being transported in the cargo hold of a C-130, a no-frills airline is first class."

"I wasn't surprised at all when I heard you'd become a fireman. You always said you wanted to become an arson investigator."

"I also said I wanted to join the military after I got my degree."

"But you dropped out of school." She flipped down the visor, exposing a small mirror so she could put on a little makeup.

"I got my degree. Six years ago, but I finished it."

"I'm glad to hear it." Puckering her lips, she applied the lip gloss, trying to ignore the pull he had over her mind and other parts.

"I've been meaning to ask. Why the Peace Corps? You never talked about that in college."

She leaned back in her seat. She could be honest, or she could lie. Her mother would tell her to fudge a little, especially if she cared about the man and wanted him in her life. Her father would tell her to be brutally honest, and if he couldn't take it, then he wasn't the man for her. What was odd, however, was that it had been her father who had an affair for years, so his advice didn't float.

Well, it did, just not coming from him.

"I'd planned on going back in high school, but then you and I happened, and I figured you'd be joining the Air Force after college and having both of us living in faraway places wouldn't make for a solid foundation for a life together."

"What?" He snapped his head in her direction as he exited the highway toward the airport. "You would have given that up just because of my plans?"

"Not your plans. Our plans."

"But you never told me about this dream."

"I wanted you more than I wanted the Peace Corps," she admitted.

"But not enough to come after me when I left."

Talk about brutal, though it wasn't the honest truth. "We could go back and forth all day on who didn't chase after whom. I thought you'd come back to school, and when I walked into the apartment we rented for our senior year, I assumed you'd be there. But you never showed up and that said a lot."

"I suppose it does, but maybe my leaving just

opened the door for you to go back to what you really wanted."

"Are you trying to pick a fight with me?" All morning he'd waffled between being nice, but standoffish, or acting like he'd been annoyed by everything about her being on his boat.

The car rolled to a stop at the rental return.

"No. I'm just trying to understand because so many of your actions contradict each other." He stepped from the vehicle, giving the attendant the keys before grabbing his suitcase from the back seat.

So did his, but she wasn't about to continue this ridiculous conversation any further. They walked into the airport in a chilly silence that made her skin prickle. She glanced his way a few times, but he looked straight ahead. He did that when he was either pondering something or annoyed.

She figured right now he was both.

"We go through the main security, then we get a bus over to the small airplane hangar. The crew is on the jet and ready to go."

"I haven't flown on a plush, private jet since my dad took the golf team to the Bahamas."

"Do you still get to play?" she asked, stepping into the airport security line through pre-check, grateful the conversation shifted quickly and easily.

"I play when I can. How about you?" He dumped his bag on the conveyor belt and stepped through the metal detector. He didn't look back as she followed suit.

She gathered her things and headed toward the bus terminal. "Not since the last time with you."

"Well, maybe we should play a round at the club while I'm home. I've always enjoyed the way you cock your hip right before you swing."

She stepped through the door he held open and climbed up on the bus. Her stomach pitched and rolled. And here he thought her actions were conflicting. He sent her one mixed message after the other, and it felt more like watching a tennis match than having a conversation.

"That right there is why I don't play."

"It's even better when you bend over to pick up your ball."

"All right. That's enough." She let out a long sigh. "You go from being pissy about what I did or didn't do years ago to flirting with me. We had our fun last night to bring us closure. Either close it, or...or...just fucking close it, okay?"

"Why don't you tell me how you really feel." He held the bar in the center of the bus over sitting next to her. "Oh, wait. You don't know how you really feel."

"Well, neither do you."

The rest of the ride went in silence, as did boarding his father's jet. She'd chosen to fly with a skeleton crew: pilot and co-pilot. This seemed to make Hunter insanely happy as he poured himself a scotch on the rocks before take-off. In all the years she'd known him, she'd never seen him drink before at least noon, and that was only when they had a football party or major family gathering.

She opted for coffee.

He leaned back in the seat across from her, swirling his drink, the ice cubes clinking against the glass. The plane leveled out, and the captain came over the loudspeaker, letting them know the estimated time of arrival and the current weather in Maryland.

"I'm sorry," Hunter said, still staring at his drink. "I'm nervous about being around family, and I'm taking it out on you."

"Thank you, but it's more than that. You've been upset with me ever since I stepped from your bedroom this morning." She fluffed her hair as if that would give her a shot of confidence. "I don't regret what happened, but I'd understand if you did."

"That's not it at all." He set the glass down and looked directly at her. "I'm glad we had last night. We couldn't get past our stubbornness back then, but we each did things to remind ourselves of what we didn't fight for, and I find myself wanting more of it, only your life is up here and mine's with the Air Force, and neither one of us is going to change that."

"What do you mean?" She clutched the leaf pendant dangling from her neck, fingering the silver piece of jewelry. She wasn't so sure she wanted the answer, but she needed it.

"We held onto each other in different ways, but we went about the lives we both wanted to live. We didn't really think twice about it. It's like we felt guilty over choosing our goals, so we tortured ourselves with constant reminders. We need to choose one, and I think we both know what that will be, no matter how badly we want a repeat."

She stared at him for a long moment, digesting his words. She wanted to argue that they were immature and young. That they didn't have the skill set to deal with what happened in their lives, but deep down, she knew he had a valid point. Only, he failed to comprehend that she would have never become a Peace Corps Volunteer had he not left her. Sure, she would have found some way to do service work, though it would have been local. Or wherever he was stationed. And there could have been opportunities in the military for her passion to help others.

But what would be the point in telling him that now when it was painfully obvious he didn't want her in his life.

"I get it and agree."

"I'm sorry if this is hurting you," he said.

Now she just wanted to throttle him. "I'm not hurt. I think it's good we talked before landing in Baltimore."

"Are we getting a car service, or is someone picking us up?"

"Your father and his wife."

"I've never met her," he said, dropping his head back.

"She's a nice lady and makes your father happy."

"How does she feel about my dad taking care of his ex-wife?" Every word was laced with a bit of kick as if they'd been drenched in Tabasco sauce.

"She's actually taking care of the day to day things, spending her days with your mom, cooking and cleaning."

"That's just weird."

"So is the fact that you had sex last night with your step-sister."

CHAPTER 5

Hunter followed Claire across the tarmac toward a stretch limo, doing his best to forget her comment about step-siblings. He knew she was just trying to mess with him because he could tell she wasn't buying his line of crap.

And it was crap.

At this point, he'd say anything to build up the wall he should have never let her tear down. His heart had taken a mini beating the moment he opened his eyes this morning to see her sprawled out on top of him in his bed. Her long hair flowing across his chest. Her arms and legs tangled up with his. Visions of leisurely walks along the beach, children frolicking in the ocean waves, maybe even a dog chasing a Frisbee, teased his mind.

The back door of the limo opened, and his father stepped out into the humid air. His hair had thinned and greyed, but his muscular frame filled out his dress slacks and shirt exactly as Hunter had remembered. His father held out his hand as a woman stepped from the vehicle. She wore a stunning light blue pantsuit. Her short brown hair was perfectly styled. From a distance, he couldn't even fathom a guess at her age, but from the few talks he'd had with his father and siblings, she was in her early sixties.

"Judy is her name, right?" he whispered. His palms grew clammy, and his pulse jackhammered in his chest.

"That's correct," Claire said, slowing her pace, resting her hand in the crook of his elbow. Instinctively, he raised his forearm. "She was married to a banker for twenty years."

"Do I have more step-siblings I need to be aware of?"

Claire let out a soft laugh. "No. She never had children."

"Why'd she get divorced?"

"She didn't. She was widowed."

He swallowed. That was good information to know, otherwise he might go and make an ass of himself by saying something stupid.

The last ten paces, he took deep calming breaths.

"Dad," he said, extending his hand.

"Hunter." His father pushed his hand aside and pulled him in for a tight and slightly-too-long hug. "You look good, boy."

"So do you, Dad."

"Claire. Dear Claire. Thanks for talking him into coming home."

"My pleasure," Claire said.

"Judy. I'd like you to meet my son, Hunter." His father beamed with pride just like he had the day Hunter had graduated from high school. His father had always been his biggest supporter, even when Hunter said no to a prep school offer to play golf and even a chance to go professional. While Hunter loved the sport, he didn't want to make it his living, no matter how good at it he was, and he was still a scratch golfer. Not bad for a guy who only played on weekends, and not every weekend because that would cut into his fishing.

"Nice to meet you, ma'am."

She took the hand he extended, but leaned in for an awkward hug. "Please don't call me ma'am, or Mrs. Jackson, because that would be more awkward than this. Judy is just fine."

A nervous laugh trickled out of his mouth. "I'm sorry I was unable to make the wedding. I really was overseas on deployment." There was no reason he needed to qualify that and by the wrinkled brow on his father's head, Hunter had not only insulted him by implying they didn't believe his response, but it also reminded everyone that Hunter hadn't been home in ten years.

"Thank you for your service," Judy said with a poised smile.

He wanted to hate the woman as much as he resented his parents for destroying what he believed had been the perfect marriage. The perfect family.

"You're welcome." His heart ached for what once was and what a fool he'd been. He hadn't chased after Claire because he wanted to follow his dream. No. He didn't stay to make it work because he was afraid, and he made it impossible for her to come after him.

He swallowed. Hard.

But his parents had betrayed him, a thought that still burned a hole in his gut. Even now, he could perfectly recall the day he'd found his mother with Mr. Thompson. A son, no matter the age, doesn't unsee something like that. He wondered if he'd found out some other way, and didn't have to be the one to tell his father, if he would have reacted differently.

He slipped into the limo, Claire sitting next to him, his father and Judy sitting across. His lungs burned with every breath he took. His father, and his father's wife were strangers to him. He had no idea what to say, much less how to act.

"Your father tells me you're a Senior Firefighter for the Air Force." She patted his father's leg. "Gerry, didn't you say it was called Fire Protection Specialist?"

His father nodded, staring at Hunter with questioning eyes, though what they questioned, Hunter didn't know.

"He also tells me you're in some training or school to be an arson investigator. That must be fascinating."

Hunter arched a brow. "How'd you know about that, Dad?"

"You've forgotten I have some high-ranking friends in the military."

"Keeping tabs on me?"

Claire pinched him, and he flinched, though not necessarily at the physical pain.

He deserved more of a pinch since the words

tumbled out of his mouth before he could think about how they would sound.

"Sorry, Dad. That's not what I meant." He rubbed the side of his leg and laced his fingers through Claire's.

She tried to pull back, but he didn't let her. He needed her warmth and her strength if he was going to get through this without being too much of an ass.

"You sort of meant it like that. I was always up your ass about everything when you were a teenager and worse when you went to college." His father smiled, shaking his head. "Remember when I tried to bribe your academic advisor to give me your grades when you refused to sign off on them?"

"You were a bit of a control freak." The corner of Hunter's mouth twitched into a smile. "I purposely maintained a status quo average just to annoy you."

"I know. Smart ass kid," his father said.

"I know an adult who is just like that," Judy said with a bright smile.

It was going to be impossible to hate the woman. She seemed perfect for his dad.

A long, thick silence filled the limo. Hunter looked out the window as they pulled into a familiar neighborhood. Not his old one, or Claire's, since his mom and her dad had bought a new place together, but it was only a couple of neighborhoods away and still within the country club. That had to be awkward at the Holiday Ball.

"Thanks for coming," his father said with a throaty tone, his eyes glossed over, threatening to tear. "I won't pretend to understand how you felt ten years ago. I had my own pain to grapple with, and I don't think I was a very good father to you or your siblings during the divorce. But I know what this will mean to your mother."

"She doesn't know I'm coming?"

Claire squeezed his hand. "She's been asking for you, and we all said we'd try to find you, but we didn't want to get her hopes up."

"I hope I don't give her a heart attack," Hunter mumbled.

"That's not funny," his father said, though there was a lightness to the words.

"It's inappropriately funny." Hunter coughed, nearly choking on the phrase his mother used to toss out whenever the locker room talk got out of hand, or a sexist joke would be told in front of her.

The limo pulled into a house on the fifth tee box. "They bought old man Walker's place?"

"You didn't know that?" Claire questioned.

"There are a lot of things I don't know," he admitted, his insides fluttering like a dog's tail. "I know this is no excuse, but the first four years I was gone, I was always in training or deployed. Even after that, I volunteered for deployment and special operations."

"So we've been told." His father's voice boomed with pride once again.

Hunter snapped his head, catching his father's gaze. Hunter expected a lecture on how easy it was in today's age to maintain contact, not genuine delight from a man who seemed to relish in his son's accomplishments, even if from a distance.

"Why don't I go see how Louisa is doing?" Judy pushed open the limo door. "Should I prepare her for Hunter's visit?"

"No," his father said, maintaining eye contact with Hunter. "I'd like it if you told her you came to see her on your own. You can tell her I sent Claire to talk you into it if you want. But, just remember, when someone knows the end is near, they look back over their lives and all the regrets and pain that comes with it, and it haunts their existence." He leaned over, putting a strong hand on Hunter's knee. "What she did was wrong, and it hurt us all. This is no excuse, but our marriage had been over for years. We stayed together for you kids. Maybe that was a big mistake."

Hunter couldn't stand to listen to reason for a second longer. "I'm here. Let's just leave it at that." He stepped from the limo, the warm sun hitting his face. Golf carts rolled across the cart path. The sound of an iron hitting a ball played like music in his ears. He ducked his head back into the limo. "What are the chances I could get a round of golf in after I visit with Mom?"

"I'll set it up."

"Thanks." He turned and faced old man Walker's house, now his mother's house. "Well, here goes nothing."

He stuffed his hands in his pockets and stood at the front door. Did he knock? Ring the doorbell? Walk in? Thankfully, he didn't have to make that decision as Judy appeared and opened the front door.

"She's awake and knows something is up, but I doubt she knows you're here."

"Can I ask you a question?" He actually had a million of them, but many would just serve to piss off everyone.

"What is it?" Judy stepped back, waving a hand into a sitting room to the right of the foyer. He recognized the white sofa from Claire's parents' house, but only because they'd had sex on it once.

Or twice.

Pictures lined the wall-to-ceiling bookcases of both families. It was strange to see his family portrait, with both his parents in it, displayed next to one of Claire's with all of her siblings and parents.

"If you've more than one, why don't we sit."

He shook his head, reaching for the frame that had a dozen small pictures of him and Claire growing up as kids.

"Your mother has an entire collection of picture frames like that one all throughout the house. She's still holding out for a reunion with the two of you."

Maybe he should tell his mother that his love for Claire would be forever tainted because of her actions, and they'd get back together when hell froze over.

God, he was a mess. One minute he wanted nothing more than to be with Claire. The next he just wanted to continue to hurt everyone.

Mostly himself.

Living a tormented life had become the only way he knew how to survive.

Being in this house, surrounded by images of family and love made him want to go running and screaming naked through the neighborhood like a crazy person. But the worst part was that he was a grown man, not a child, and he had no right to begrudge his parents happiness. Or to judge their decisions.

"I hope you don't mind if I'm blunt," he said.

"I'm your mother's primary caregiver, I'm used to blunt."

He let out a short laugh. "How do you do it? I mean, taking care of your husband's ex-wife. That's got to be hard."

"It might have been if I knew them during the divorce, but I didn't. I only saw two people who stopped loving each other but never stopped loving their kids." Judy ran her fingers across an old Victorian desk. "Your parents have become friends. Close friends. I'd be a bitch if I stood between two people who have shared so much joy and heartache." She closed the gap, reaching out and curling her fingers around his biceps. "They became close over their shared grief of hurting and losing you. They both love you very much, but they are about as stubborn as a baby that is unwilling to walk."

"That they are."

"Anything else?"

"Just point me in the direction of my mother," he said. If he didn't do this now, he'd never do.

"Upstairs and down the hallway. You'll walk right

into the master bedroom. I should warn you, she's weak and doesn't look well. She's lost a ton of weight and is quite pale."

"That has to drive her insane. She always loved a good tan."

"She demands tanning lotion every day."

"That sounds like my mother." He left Judy standing in the sitting room as he climbed the staircase. The hallway walls were filled with more photos and familiar furniture from both his childhood home and Claire's.

I slept with my step-sister.

Well, she was his girlfriend before that, and it didn't matter anyway.

He raised his trembling hand and knocked on the door.

"Come in," his mother's voice rang out as soft and sweet as he remembered. At nine years old, he'd broken his wrist snow skiing on a family vacation. It had been displaced and had to be reset. His mother talked to him through the entire process, telling him stories of her childhood and the crazy things his grandfather used to do.

He sucked in a deep breath and told himself this would be easier than running into a burning building.

Right.

He stepped through door, mentally preparing himself. "Hey, Ma," he said as she came into view. She was propped up in her bed, a food tray over her legs. Her once long, thick hair had thinned and turned grey. She wasn't as pale as he thought she'd be, but her frail body sucker-punched his ability to take another step.

She turned her head, raising a small sandwich. Her hand fell to the tray, sending the plate with the rest of the food onto the bed.

He raced to her side, quickly cleaning up the mess, thankful no liquid had been spilled. He set her food off to the side and sat on the edge of the bed. "Surprise?" He didn't think his heart could ache more, but seeing his strong, sophisticated mother in such a vulnerable state drove home how much he'd missed out on during the last ten years.

She blinked a few times, shaking her head. "Now I'm delusional," she whispered.

"No. I'm really here." He took his mother's feeble hand in his, rubbing gently.

"I can't decide if I should hug you or slap you."

"How about both?"

She raised her arm and patted the side of his

cheek. "If you weren't so damned pretty, I'd really smack you."

He leaned in, drawing his mother close, being careful not to hurt her, but she had other things in mind as she nearly crushed him with a hug and slobbered on his cheek with a million pecks like she used to do when he was a small boy and he'd run away trying to brush them off, totally embarrassed she'd done that in front of his friends.

"You need to shave." His mother leaned back, folding her arms over her chest.

"I didn't have much time this morning. We just landed less than an hour ago."

"Claire got you to come home." Her mother waggled a finger under his nose. "And don't lie to me. I'm not that fragile, and I'm not dead yet."

He swallowed the sob that smacked the back of his throat and willed the tears glossing over his eyes to fade away. "She had something to do with it."

"Your father sent her. He doesn't think I know. He has it in his head that I needed you to come home on your own. But screw that. I'll take it any way I can. Besides, you and Claire belong together. Oh, the babies you two will make. They will be spectular."

He shook his head. "I didn't think you could get

any more candid, but you have and you've developed a very dry sense of humor."

"Losing your son, then your second husband, and now dying, will do that to a woman."

"You didn't lose me," he mumbled, wondering if she was trying to hurt him, or just being inappropriately honest.

"Yeah. Actually, I did. After I got the last letter you sent me a year after you'd left, I realized how badly I handled the situation and that you would never forgive me. And don't go saying that you do just because you think it's what a dying woman wants to hear because it's not. I just wanted to see you and have the chance to tell you I'm sorry. In person."

"Apology accepted." He leaned in and kissed her cheek. Even in death, she still smelled like roses. "I'm sure I owe you a few."

"You owe Claire a lot more than me." His mother tilted her head slightly to the left, pursing her lips, giving him that look that dared him to argue with her.

"We talked."

"And?"

"There is no and. Claire and I were over a long time ago. We've both moved on."

"Really? Do you have a girlfriend?"

He opened his mouth, but she didn't let him speak.

"I bet you don't, and if you lie to me I'll know it."

"I've had girlfriends."

"But they don't last, do they> And neither do Claire's."

"I can't speak for her, but I'm deployed more than I'm home most years, and that doesn't make for a happy girlfriend."

"Because they aren't right for you. She is, and I'm going to get the two of you back together if it's the last thing I do."

"I'm sorry, Ma, but it's not going to happen. Claire and I talked about it at length." Okay, a little white lie since they had simply brushed over the topic.

"Talk is cheap. How long are you here for?"

"Couple of days. But I'll come back as often as I can." Words he hadn't expected to come out of his mouth, but he meant them.

"I need you to do me a favor."

"Whatever you need," he said, thankful they were off the Claire topic.

"While you're here, take Claire out on a couple of dates. See how—"

"Mom. Do you really want to start a fight on my first day back in ten years?"

She straightened her spine, sitting up taller. "No. That's why you're just going to take her out. It won't kill you. If after a few dates, nothing is there, no harm done."

Little did his mother know that his heart was already bleeding out.

"And it will make a dying woman happy."

"Fine," he said a little too quickly, but it put a smile on his mother's face and he preferred that to a scowl.

"Good. Now why don't you go play some golf with your father, and we can all have dinner together tonight. Then, you can take Claire out for drinks, or a movie, or maybe a romantic stroll."

He kissed his mother's cheek, helping her fluff her pillow as she shifted lower in the bed. He snagged the food tray and headed for the stairs with a funny tickle across his skin. It wasn't an unpleasant feeling, but it certainly was an unwelcoming one.

When he got to the bottom of the stairs and rounded the corner, he was greeted by Claire and his father.

"How'd things go?" his father asked.

"It was interesting. She forgives me, but she certainly knows how to play the dying card."

"What the hell does that mean?" Claire asked, snapping her hip to the side in an indignant gesture.

"She knew Dad sent you to get me, and her dying wish wasn't for my forgiveness, but for the two of us to get back together and while I'm here, I've been ordered to date you."

His father bent over laughing.

"I don't see what is so funny," Hunter said, scowling.

"Your mother always gets her way." His father glanced between Hunter and Claire. "And she's always right."

CHAPTER 6

"I'm glad for this time alone with you."

Hunter took the glass of scotch his father offered and settled into one of the outdoor chairs in front one of three fire pits. The evening sun lowering toward the horizon.

"I know this took a lot for you to come home," his father said, staring into his glass, swirling the dark liquid. "I appreciated as much as your mother does."

"If I'm being honest, I'm glad I'm here. It's awkward as hell, but I think I would have regretted not coming."

"I'm glad to hear that."

He stared at his father, studying every line on his

face, noticing the way he sipped his drink, realizing Hunter did it exactly the same way.

"Are you happy, dad?"

"Not completely, no. You cutting us all off has taken a toll on that." His father held up a hand. "I don't blame you for that and I can't imagine what it must have been like for you, but the pain of knowing your son is a phone call away, and he won't answer, well, that has hurt. A lot."

"But you lived your life. Got re-married."

"And look at you," his father said with a wave of his hand. "You've become a mighty fine man, but are you happy?"

He sipped his drink, letting the burn of the alcohol glide across his throat. "I'm not unhappy."

His father let out a short laugh. "I know you think you're mother's nuts for wanting you and Claire to date for the time you are here. She feels responsible for your break-up. Always has. And you know, Claire's father felt the same way."

Hunter breathed slowly. "I can't help it, whenever I look back, I'm still angry and Claire didn't seem to care what my mother's was doing to our family."

"Of course she cared, but, because she stuck

around, she saw how jovial her father had become and over time, we all developed an odd friendship. Truthfully, if I had let your mother go when you were just a small boy, none of this would have happened. She was miserable with me, and I with her. Our lives had become something entirely different, but we decided, that splitting up the family would be bad for you kids."

"It was bad for me." Hunter raised his glass in a sarcastic cheers.

"That's where you refuse to see the bigger picture. Had we divorced back then, you and Claire night have never happened and she was the best damn thing that ever happened to you. I agree with your mother. You need to give you and Claire a second chance."

Hunter set his glass on the table and stood. "No offense, Dad, but you don't know me. I'm not the same man who walked away."

"But I know Claire."

Hunter shook his head. "Perhaps, but I don't really know any of you anymore, so I'd appreciate it if you'd back off the Claire thing. "I'll take Claire out for mom, but I won't pretend I still have feelings for her."

Actually, he'd have to pretend not to have any feelings for her, at least to himself.

Claire smoothed down the front of her miniskirt, doing a one-hundred-eighty degree turn in front of the mirror. Louisa had been kind enough to let her keep some of her things in the bedroom she'd called home between college and her travels with the Peace Corps before getting her own apartment in Bethesda. Since Louisa had gotten sick, Claire had made a point of coming home every weekend and tried to make it home for dinner at least once a week.

Gathering her hair and holding it behind her head, she contemplated putting it up.

Hunter preferred it down.

She reached for a ponytail holder and a clip. Twisting her hair, she pulled it back, leaving a few strands out to fan her face. Satisfied that Hunter would hate her outfit and her hair, she left the comfort of her bedroom and made her way downstairs. Dinner would certainly prove to be interesting to say the very least. She knew Louisa would play matchmaker, but what she didn't count on was Hunter's willingness to play along.

Keyword: Play.

"Don't you look stunning," Louisa said, sitting at

the head of the table in the dining room, her IV drip perched next to her. Louisa did her best to look as pretty as possible by wearing a little makeup, styling what hair she had left, and wearing designer shawls to cover her comfortable pajamas that didn't give her bed sores. Most nights she actually ate in her room with Judy, or a staff nurse, or one of her friends that came to visit. But when the family showed up, she did her best to make it to the dinner table.

"She's always the prettiest girl in the room," Judy said, sitting to the left of Louisa, Gerry in the seat to the right.

The table sat ten comfortably, and her father had always sat at the opposite end, but no one ever sat there now and the wait staff never set a place setting.

Claire wasn't quite sure where to sit. Most dinners included other family members, or she usually sat next to Judy, but what if Hunter wanted to be across from his father.

"This is all wrong," Louisa said, waving her arms frantically. "Judy, dear. You should be sitting next to your adoring husband so the two lovebirds can play footsie under the table."

Swallowing the sarcastic remark, Claire took her seat, leaving a space between her and Hunter's mother, while Judy scurried across the room to be by

Gerry. If someone had told Claire ten years ago that she'd be forced to date Hunter, she would have laughed hysterically at the absurdity of it. She'd loved him back then, so she thought they'd be together forever.

Now she just wanted to get this over with. She figured maybe three or four dates, and they'd be able to say they'd given it the good old college try.

"Where is the prodigal son?" Claire asked.

Louisa gasped.

"I didn't mean it that way." But she really had. Her frustration level was at the breaking point. One more cutest couple comment, and she'd blow up like the Fourth of July.

"Are you sure about that?" Hunter's voice startled her, making her jump.

She looked over her shoulder. He leaned against the doorjamb sporting a pink button-down shirt, black slacks, and a pair of dark boat shoes. He'd always been the best dressed person in any room. Not to mention the hottest. Girls drooled over him, constantly trying to get him to notice them, but during all the years they dated, he never once turned his head.

"There he is." His mother patted the chair next to her. "Judy poured a nice bottle of red. I can't have any, but if I recall correctly, you had your father's taste for wine."

"I still do." Hunter sauntered across the room, eyeing her with a devilish twinkle in his eye like the night he'd taken her to a fancy restaurant and then made love to her on the beach, listening the waves crash against the sand.

She hated that look. It always meant he was up to something.

"I also still hate your hair like this." He snagged the clip holding her hair up before tugging at her ponytail.

"Ouch." She balked, but he'd always been good at taking her hair out of an up-do without pulling the strands out. "I can't believe you just did that."

He tossed her accessories on the hutch on the other side of the room. "You knew I would, which is why you wore your hair that way."

Louisa scowled. "Children."

"I wore it that way because I don't like eating my hair," she said, trying to diffuse the situation. The last thing she wanted to do was upset his mother, though that was his doing, not hers.

He looped his arm over her chair, leaning in, his hot breath warming her skin. "You just wanted my fingers in it again," he whispered, but not soft enough because his mother's frown turned to a smile wider than the state of Texas.

When Louisa left the table, Claire was going to lay into Hunter. It was one thing to date for the benefit of his mother, but it was entirely another thing to turn it into a display that would get her hopes up.

"Stop it," she said behind gritted teeth, kicking him under the table.

He took that as it was okay to pat her thigh.

She glared at him with a smile. "What's for dinner tonight?" she asked, turning her attention to his mother.

"I had the cook make Hunter's favorite." Louisa rang the bell on the table. A little old-fashioned, but the staff didn't seem to mind.

"Oh, I love blackened salmon," his father said, raising his glass. "I'd like to make a toast."

This should be rich.

She held her wine up, waiting to down it in one gulp.

"To family." He lifted his arm higher.

"That's it?" Louisa asked.

"I think that says it all," Gerry said.

"I'll drink to that." She didn't bother to clink with anyone. The red, tart liquid burned as it flowed from her throat to her stomach. She wasn't even sure if she actually swallowed, much less tasted anything. "I'm ready for another."

Everyone at the table stared at her with a perfectly arched brow.

Thankfully, Hunter filled her glass, though not as high as she would have liked, but really, she needed to slow down and get a grip. It was all just fake dating.

The courses came and went, and the conversation seemed to stay off whether or not she and Hunter were made for each other. She enjoyed listening to Hunter's tales from his service in the military, though he did say, 'I can't talk about that,' a lot.

By the time the after-dinner coffee was served, but before dessert, it was obvious to everyone that Louisa was exhausted, even though she kept trying to say she was fine.

"Let's get you up to bed," Gerry said.

"You should be saying that to your current wife, not your ex-wife."

He smiled. "As soon as we get you upstairs, I plan on taking her home and to—"

"Dad," Hunter said with a scrunched nose. "This is just too werid for me."

Gerry laughed.

"I'll help." Judy rose, helping Louisa to her feet.

"Goodnight, son." Louisa hugged Hunter.

A warmth spread over Claire's heart seeing Hunter embrace his mother again. She really needed to relax and just get with his mother's program for the week.

"I've had the staff make the bed in the room next to Claire's. I think you'll be comfortable there."

Claire coughed, burning her lips on the hot coffee she'd just brought to her lips. "That's a shared bathroom."

"I know. I didn't want the cleaning people to have to deal with another one. This is just easier." Louisa patted her shoulder. "Stop fighting it, dear. Trust me. By the end of the week, you're going to realize how madly in love you two still are."

She opened her mouth, but snapped it shut. Nothing good would come from saying exactly what she was thinking. Leaning across the table, she took the second bottle of wine that had been opened and poured herself a hearty glass. Once Louisa was out of the room, she turned to look at Hunter. "Cheers." She chugged half of it. "I should have left when you shut the cabin door on me."

"I would have still come." He joined her in more vino.

"Okay, but we wouldn't have had sex last night, which opened up this crazy can of worms."

"My mother doesn't know we had sex. She's just—"

"I do now," Louisa said, pushing her IV pole through the dining room. "I forgot my cheaters. Can't see a damn thing without them."

Claire dropped her head to the table and groaned. A wave a nausea flowed from her toes to her brain.

"You might as well share a room. I have no issue with that out of wed—"

"Louisa," Gerry said sternly. "Leave them alone."

"Good idea," Hunter said, sipping his wine like a gentlemen.

Claire kept her head down, breathing deeply so she didn't hyperventilate from embarrassment. It was worse than getting caught with her hand in Hunter's pants when they'd been in high school.

"Everyone's gone." Hunter brushed her hair to the side, tracing his finger across her neck. "I'm sorry, but I thought you'd want to keep the tattoo to yourself."

"They've all seen it. Made their comments."

"So, I just made it all worse."

She bolted upright. "It wasn't just the letting my hair down thing, but you made a sexual innuendo—"

"I know. I'm sorry. It's just that it does really make my mother happy, and I've come to realize I've caused her so much pain. I kind of want to make it up to her."

"I'm glad. Really I am, but please, leave me out of it."

"Come on. Let's take this outside and sit by the pool." He snagged the bottle of red. "We can discuss a plan that will satisfy my mother's need for us to be together, but with the boundaries you want."

"We're going to have to fake date until she dies, and this goes under the inappropriate category, but I think you coming home might have extended her life indefinitely."

He laced his fingers through hers.

She told herself it was just practice. The only problem with that was how much she liked practicing.

"We only have to date when I'm home, and I don't have a lot of leave time. I'm also scheduled to deploy in a month for about six weeks, but I might see if I can get a family medical leave from that and have it postponed."

She glanced up at him. "You'd do that for your mother?"

"I was wrong to cut her out."

She plopped herself on a lounge chair, making sure her drink didn't spill, which was amazing considering now tipsy she was. Hunter was turning out to be the man she'd fallen in love with. Not the jerk that took off.

Go figure.

"Why Hunter Jackson, I think you might have grown up," she said.

"Don't tell anyone. I'd like to keep it a secret." He sat on the foot of the chair, swirling his glass. "We're going to have to been seen in public, at the club. Are you ready for that?"

"I've already gotten two texts congratulating me on our recent reunion."

He shook his head. "I played golf with Eddy and his dad, both asking when the wedding will be."

"What have we gotten ourselves into?"

CHAPTER 7

Hunter spent the first night in his mother's house tossing and turning. Every time he got up to use the bathroom, he hoped he'd run into Claire, but it never happened.

And he couldn't bring himself to sneak into her room. Things had gotten too weird. He needed to spend some time alone with her, without the premise of making his mother happy. So, with that in mind, he'd borrowed a buddy's sailboat, and he and Claire would spend the day on the Chesapeake before being put on display at the club during an annual Tuesday evening couples' night, golf and all.

"You and boats," she said as he stepped on the twenty-foot day sailor. "You should have joined the Navy."

"Their firefighter program isn't as intense as the Air Force."

"Perhaps, but their white dress uniforms are smoking hot."

"You women love a man in uniform." He untied the boat after starting the single engine. It wasn't the windiest day, and he probably wouldn't even put the sail up. Hell, floating and drinking a few beers seemed more like a plan than anything else.

She'd taken off her T-shirt, showing off a tiny bikini top. The sexy miniskirt made the outfit complete. Talk about smoking hot. She burned his lips every time he kissed her. She never understood how sexy she was, even now. She might carry herself with confidence, but that came because she knew she was smart. In the looks department, she always saw herself as just another pretty girl, nothing special.

She was special in every way.

"How was breakfast with your mother?" she asked, leaning back on the bench on the starboard side.

"She was disappointed you didn't join us."

"I went to yoga class, like I do every day I'm at her house." She covered her eyes with her hand, glancing in his direction. “Did she bring up the sleeping arrangements?”

“And then some.” He shook his head. “My mom was always direct. Hell, she made me blush giving me the sex talk, trying to explain why I should listen to what a woman wanted and if that wasn’t bad enough, she gave a few graphic details about how to please a woman. I wanted to crawl in a hole and die.”

“Well, you must have listened to her, because you always done what I wanted and from the start, you knew what to do.”

He laughed. “You never gave me a choice. Always so demanding in bed.”

“I most certainly am not.”

“Whatever you say.” He steered the boat out into the Chesapeake, enjoying the hot summer sun beating down on his face. Not much different than being at home, except for Claire, only he felt as if she belonged with him out on the boat.

That was a crazy thought.

He pulled the throttle back, slowing the boat into an alcove they used to hang out in back in the day. “Let’s relax here.” He shut the engine down and tossed over the anchor, securing the boat between a half-dozen other boats enjoying the day.

“Wow, this brings back memories,” she said as

she smoothed out two towels. “We had a lot of fun here.”

“We sure did.” He sat down next to her and opened the cooler. “Look at all the kids in these boats.”

“I know. We look like a couple of old farts.”

“We are old farts.” He twisted off the cap from a Corona light and handed it to her.

“Why’d you bring me here?”

“It seemed like a nice place to spend the day and talk without being scrutinized by everyone our parents know.” He leaned back on his elbows

“Speaking of parents, my mother texted, and she’s bringing her new boyfriend to the club tonight.”

“Great. She never liked me much.” Before the affair, he’d gotten along with Mr. Thompson well enough, but Mrs. Thompson terrified him.

Claire sipped her beer, lifting her head toward the sun. “She doesn’t like anyone who’s penis I’ve touched.”

He raised his longneck. “I don’t like those pricks either.”

She clanked her bottle with his. “I’m not fond of all the felines you’ve had your hands on.”

The strange turn of events his life had taken over

the last twenty-four hours felt more like the Twilight Zone than reality. "So, we're both jealous and miserable, relationship-wise, and yet we're more awkward with each other than that pimply teenaged boy over there trying to feel up the blond who seems so into him, only he's too hormonal to know it."

"Oh my God. That's almost exactly what I said to you when I first kissed you."

"My mother always liked how aggressive you were, which still weirds me out."

Claire tilted her head and peered over her sunglasses.

"Well, you were aggressive," he said.

"Only in response to you," she whispered, brushing her hair from her face. "I'm sorry about your mom. I wish things were different."

"So do I," he admitted. His mother's illness had been another reason that had kept him up the night before.

His mother had put on a brave front, but after talking with her doctor this morning, Hunter had a much better idea of how sick his mother really was. She had days, or at best, a couple of weeks before her organs went into failure. The cancer had eaten up all of her insides, leaving her with nothing but sickness.

"What are you thinking about?"

"I've missed out on so much. My sister is still mad as hell at me, but says she'll be coming over tomorrow night for dinner. My brother and his family are coming too, which will be nice."

"That will really make your mother happy. I'll make sure I have plans."

"Not a good idea. My mom wants you there. I actually think she believes we'll make the announcement of our engagement."

"That would give MY mother a heart attack."

"Doesn't she know this is all fake dating? That we are just pretending for the sake of my mother?"

Claire shook her head, biting down on her lower lip. Never a good sign.

"Wonderful. So, she thinks we're getting back together as well."

"I'd be lying if I didn't say she's hopeful. She thinks my dating record has gone downhill since you, which is funny, considering she used to tell me I could do better than you."

He winked. "Boyfriends don't come any better than me."

She cocked her head. "You're a conceited ass." She slapped his shoulder, letting her fingers linger over their shared tattoo.

"Oh, for fuck's sake. I can't take it anymore." He pointed to the kids on the boat next to them. The young boy kept trying to get closer to the girl on the deck. "We need to give that boy a hand."

"How do you suppose we do that?"

Hunter whistled. "Hey. Do either of you have a cell phone we can use? Ours are dead, and I need to let a buddy of ours know where we are."

Claire leaned closer. "What are you doing?" she whispered.

"Helping a brother out."

"Sure," the boy yelled.

Hunter dove into the water, swimming toward the kid's boat. Hopefully, he'd read the notes on his phone that Hunter would leave about dating, or at the very least, look at the texts Hunter would send his way once he got the kids number.

"I really appreciate this," Hunter said as he pushed himself up, sitting on the stern swim platform, taking the phone the boy offered. "Your phone or hers?"

"Mine," the boy said, glancing over his shoulder.

The young girl lay on the bow with ear buds, her feet tapping away. First Hunter punched in his number, sending himself a text, then he opened the notes tab on the phone.

You want help with making a move on the girl? Just watch and follow what I do.

He handed the phone back, with the notes facing the boy who squinted and gave Hunter a funny look. Jumping back into the water, he realized he must have really looked like a creeper, but hopefully the boy would take notice.

Hunter dove back into the water. The cool feel of the ocean rolled over his skin. He eyed Claire, who sat, hugging her knees, smiling at him.

God, what a fool he'd been for ten fucking years.

"Seriously, what did you do?" Claire asked, handing him a towel.

"I told him to follow exactly what I do, so whatever you do, don't hit me and when I lean in to kiss you, make it look good."

"I don't think I can do that. I mean, you're such a terrible kisser."

He smiled, but what he really wanted to do was draw her in by her hips and plant a wet one on her right now, but he'd have to wait.

They sat on the bow, cross-legged, watching the

young couple, waiting for the right moment, which came when the girl sat up.

Hunter noticed the kid glancing his way, so he raised a hand, brushing a piece of hair from Claire's face, dropping his finger to her shoulder and gliding it across her skin.

"Wow, the boy's mimicking you."

"Good," he whispered, sliding his finger back up, doing a little circle on the top of her shoulder. "Too bad the kid can't hear what I'm about to whisper in your ear." He leaned in, feeling the warmth of her skin against his lips. "You're more beautiful than the sun's rays dancing over the water."

"Good line," she said.

He kissed her cheek. "You're making my heart melt."

"Oh, look, he just did what you did and...oh, wow, she's aggressive."

"What's she doing?"

"This." Claire wrapped her arms around him, smacking her mouth against his while her tongue swirled around, making him dizzy with desire.

"My job here is done." He leaned back on his hands, stretching his legs. The young couple across from them continued to kiss for a little while longer, then giggled and laughed, and kissed some more.

"I would have never thought to do that," she said.

"What? Kiss me?"

She tilted her head. "You know what I meant."

He nodded. "But you're thinking about kissing me now."

"That one beer must have gone straight to your head."

He lay on his back, staring up at her. "Maybe, but I'm hoping after our date tonight, I'll get to feel you up like I did the night of the end of the summer fireworks."

She slapped his arm. "You're impossible."

"I know." He closed his eyes, letting the rocking of the boat gently lull him. If this boat had a bed, he'd be leading her to the cuddy and using his best moves to get her to sleep with him again.

His heart wasn't melting anymore.

No. His heart burned with the need to be with her again.

To love her.

CHAPTER 8

Claire's knee jumped wildly under the table. Not even Hunter's steady hand could calm her nerves.

"That last put of yours was amazing," James, her mother's new boyfriend said.

"He was always quite the golfer," her mother said with a smile. For a woman who hadn't liked Hunter that much, she certainly had a thing for him now. "I'm so sad your father and his new bride couldn't join us."

Hunter loosened the tie around his neck before taking another large sip of wine. "My mother wasn't feeling too well, so they stayed with her."

"I'm so sorry," her mother said shaking her head. "You're mother's a good woman and I wish this wasn't happening. She's been through so much. First her son not speaking to—"

"Mom," Claire interrupted. "Can we please not go there. Hunter is her now."

"Yes. He is, and that says something." Her mother let out a long breath. "So tell me, Hunter, what exactly are your intentions with my daughter?"

"Mom, really, I'm not twelve."

"It's alright. I suspect if I had a child, I'd be the same way." Hunter set his glass down. "It's been a long time and a lot of feelings have been hurt. Right now, it's all about reconnecting. I never stopped caring for your daughter and my mother's illness has reminded me how short life is."

Claire coughed. The man could act. Really good.

Too good.

"That's all well and good, but you made my little girl cry and I'd hate to go through that again."

"Oh, my, God, mother. This has to stop. Can we just have a nice dinner and not rehash the past."

"But if you two are getting back together—"

"Mrs. Thompson." Hunter put his hand over her mothers. "I have no intention of making Claire cry. That's the last thing I want. Right now, we're simply dating, getting to know one another again. I don't know where it will lead, I just know I want the opportunity to explore the possibilities and Claire seems to want the same thing." He turned and caught her gaze. "Right. That is what you want."

Nothing like putting her on the spot with a big old hot truth, but told in the form of a lie, because Hunter was just putting on a good show.

"Yes. That's what I want."

Claire tossed her purse on the dresser then fell backward onto the soft, plush bed, exhausted for the evening with her whacko mother.

The second they'd walked in the door, Hunter had been called to see his mother. She'd had a rough day, pain-wise, but also, the day nurse said Louisa had taken a turn for the worse. Claire feared the end was sooner than everyone thought.

Louisa put on a brave face every day and was a true fighter. One of the strongest women Claire had ever known.

A couple of light knocks came from the bathroom. She rolled her head and there stood Hunter in a light-blue button-down shirt and a pair of dark slacks.

"Is your mom okay?"

"She's resting a little more comfortably right now. The doctor will be over in the morning, but he thinks we should take her to the hospital."

"She wants to stay home and die here."

"I know. I told her I wouldn't make her go." He leaned against the doorjamb. "Is that the right decision?"

"I think so." Claire scooted up to the head of the bed. "All they will do in the hospital is manage her pain, which we are doing here, but she won't have the comforts of home."

He shoved his hands in his pockets, staring at her intently.

"Something wrong?"

He sauntered across the room, kicked off his shoes and stood at the end of the bed. Curling his fingers around her ankles, he yanked her toward him. Her dress slid up her thighs and over her butt, exposing her tiny thong. Her breathing became erratic as her chest heaved. She opened her mouth, but no words came out, only a lust-filled groan.

He dropped to his knees, leaned forward, and kissed her passionately through her cotton panties.

She should stop him. He didn't want her, he wanted to bury his pain inside someone. Anyone would probably do. She understood the pain of losing a parent. When her father died, all she wanted was for someone to hold her. Love her.

She'd wanted Hunter and wished he'd come for her.

But he didn't.

He pushed the fabric to the side and slipped in two fingers. Her body was already moist with anticipation. She clung to the bed sheets, digging her heels into the mattress. Whatever he needed, she'd give it to him.

As he pulled her panties off, a ripple of heartache washed over her. She'd let him take her because she was selfish. She wanted to have him as many times as she could, no matter the cost to her heart. She tried to tell herself she was doing this for him. Helping him ease his grief of reconnecting with his mother, only to lose her in death.

He nestled himself between her legs, kissing and sucking. Her hips rolling involuntarily with the gentle gliding of his fingers. He kissed her passionately as if he were kissing her mouth. His hands massaged her thighs. His normal earnestness was replaced with tenderness. There was no desperation in his touch. No raw animal desire.

Just sweet love.

She gasped. Resisting the urge to clutch his head and grind herself against him.

His tongue floated across her like a feather drifting in the air. The room spun as an orgasm erupted inside her like a volcano. Her body trembled, and she struggled to catch her breath. He kissed her stomach, pushing himself off the bed.

She watched him undress in silence as she removed her dress, tossing it haphazardly to the floor. Their normal banter replaced with unspoken words. His gaze roamed her body like a knife gliding through a decadent piece of chocolate cake.

For the first time with him, she had no idea what to do, so she lay there, waiting, letting him take his fill of her body.

Her pulse beat out of control, and she began to wonder if he was even going to climb back on the bed and make love to her.

Make love.

The concept tore through her mind. Their sex had always been playful. It wasn't that they hadn't once loved each other, but sex wasn't necessarily how they conveyed the strong emotion with one another. It was an act of pleasure.

He finally made his way back to the bed, climbing between her legs, the length of him throbbing against her thigh. He planted his elbows next to her ears, his hands cupping her face as he stared into her eyes. Saying nothing, he slowly shifted, sinking himself into her.

She dug her fingers into his shoulders, holding on for dear life. Blinking, she managed to keep the tears stinging her eyes from breaking free.

She loved him.

Never stopped.

Never would.

But she'd never have him. Once his mother passed, he'd go back to Florida. He wouldn't ask her to come with him. She knew that for a fact. And she couldn't beg him to stay.

They were right back where they had left off ten years ago, and there would be no happy ending.

His lips brushed gently over hers as his hips rose up and down in a soft rolling motion like waves crashing at the shoreline.

Her back involuntarily arched into him, her soft moans gaining in strength. She felt every inch of him swell deep inside. Her eyes remained locked with his mesmerizing stare. Biting down on her lip, a second climax shook her and with it he tenderly kissed her lips a couple of times. His breath labored as his movements increased in both speed and intensity. His eyes widened as a deep guttural groan vibrated from his chest.

His body tightened as he thrust once, his release spilling out inside her.

No condom.

What a horrible thought to have right at this moment. She quickly pushed it aside, rubbing her hands up and down his back, rocking her hips slightly, enjoying the way his pupils dilated, then contracted as he orgasmed.

He kissed her nose and then collapsed on top of her. She gladly accepted his weight, gently stroking his shoulders.

She held him like that for another ten minutes before he rolled to his side, tucking himself up behind her, holding her in his arms. In minutes, he was fast asleep.

Closing her eyes, she let out a long breath.

"I love you," she whispered so quietly that she barely heard the words herself.

He certainly hadn't, because if had, he would have leapt from the bed and run for cover.

CHAPTER 9

Claire peeked open her eyes, the morning sunlight shining through the window. She blinked a few times, gaining focus.

"What time is it?" she asked.

No response.

She'd never been one to sleep in, and she hadn't known Hunter to either.

Stretching, she rolled over, reaching out for him and got nothing but an empty bed.

She bolted upright, clutching the covers over her bare chest.

"Hunter?" she called.

Looking around the room, she noticed his clothes had been picked up.

Her heart sank. He'd snuck out.

She'd woken up alone.

Again.

That shouldn't be an issue. He must have gotten up and decided to let her sleep. That would be the normal thing to do, not to think he'd taken off in the middle of the night.

Quickly, she got dressed in a pair of cotton shorts and a tank top. Deciding to check to see if he was in his room, she knocked on the door from inside the bathroom.

Silence.

She pushed open the door with a shaky hand and a pounding heart.

The bed was perfectly made, which she expected since he'd slept with her last night. She walked around the room and realized his suitcase was gone.

She sucked in her lower lip. A combination of rage and sorrow flowed through her body.

How could he just up and leave not just her, but his mother?

She raced through the house, making her way downstairs and into the kitchen where Gerry and Judy sat at the table, hovering over a couple mugs of coffee.

"Where's Hunter?"

"He left a note saying he had to go to Florida to

take care of something," Gerry said, glancing over his shoulder.

"When is he coming back?"

"The note said he'd be in touch," Judy said as she stood. "Can I make you some breakfast?"

She shook her head. "Be in touch? What does that mean? Does Louisa know?"

"Yes. He visited with her briefly this morning." Judy laced her fingers over Claire's biceps. "She's not doing well. The doctor just left, and he said her kidneys aren't functioning. He believes she'll slip into a coma soon."

"And Hunter left after hearing that? Unbelievable. What an asshole."

Judy jerked her hand back. "He's coming back."

"Right," Claire said in a huff. He'd left once before without every looking back. He could easily do it again. "Where is the note?"

"I tossed it," Gerry said with a questioning tone. "Honey, what's going on?"

"Nothing."

Only everything.

A tear rolled down her cheek.

"Something has your feathers in a tailspin." Gerry pulled out a chair. "Sit down and tell us what happened."

She sucked in a deep breath and leaned against the counter, wiping her face. This was not something she could do sitting down.

"I don't think I should be here when he comes back."

"Why do you say that?" Gerry asked. "Did you get into a fight?"

No. We made love. I told him I loved him, but he doesn't love me, so he bolted.

"Not a fight so much, but I don't belong here with him right now. I'm sure he sent me a text message or something asking me to leave before he gets back."

"I don't think my son would do that," Gerry said defensively.

She wanted to lay into him about how no one knew Hunter anymore and remind him of the pain Hunter had left in his wake ten years ago. "He needs time to be with you and his mom. He doesn't need me."

"What about Louisa?" Judy asked with a furrowed brow. "She would be so sad if you left."

"I'll be back to visit, but I'm going to move back into my apartment."

The room filled with a deafening silence. When Hunter had left the last time, he'd given her an ultimatum. He told her if she didn't come with him, he would never return for her, ever.

He up and left the next day.

Maybe he'd be back for his mom, but if he wanted her here, he would have woken her up and told her, or left a note, or at worst, sent her a text.

"I'm going to go visit with Louisa and then I'm going to pack my things." She straightened her spine and sucked in her pride.

Maybe getting over him would be easier the second time.

Hunter tossed his suitcase in the back of Ace's Jeep. "Thanks for picking me up."

"No problem. Nice jet."

"I prefer the metal seats in the back a C-130."

"I doubt that." Ace pulled out of the airport, heading toward the marina. "How's your mom?"

"Not well at all."

"So, why are you here instead of being with her?"

"I need to get the ring," he said, tripping on the last word. He'd woken up around three in the morning with Claire in his arms, her hair pooled over his chest, the golden locks glistening in the moonlight. His heart had been beating out of control, and all he could think about was spending the rest his life trying to make up for the past and give her everything she wanted and needed.

"What ring?"

"My mother's ring." Hunter rubbed his shaky hand over his thigh.

"I'm sorry, I don't follow."

Hunter stared out the window at the Intercoastal Waterway. He'd give up his boat and the Air Force to be with Claire. He could be a firefighter anywhere, and he wanted to be where she was. "My mother, in an attempt to get me to come home years ago, sent me her engagement ring and told me how crushed Claire had been when I left."

"So, your mom wants the ring?"

"No. It's not for my mom. It's for Claire." The bubble of fear he'd been feeling blossomed into a blooming flower.

"Why? Does your mom want her to have it?"

"For a married man, you're really fucking clueless."

Ace turned into the marina parking lot, glancing in his direction.

He smiled. "I'm going to ask Claire to marry me."

Ace let up on the clutch while still in gear,

lurching the car forward. "Well, why are you sitting here? Get your ass in gear, and I'll drive you back to the airport."

Hunter didn't waste any time, snagging his suitcase and racing down the dock like a lunatic. He didn't know when he'd come back, so he needed to pack more clothes. He'd been given leave for as long as he needed. Tears welled in his eyes. His mother wouldn't last long. Maybe a week, but hopefully she'd get to see her ring on Claire's finger.

Once on the boat, he went straight to the safe. The hole in his heart slowly mended, but a prickle of fear that she'd say no troubled him deeply. He also had to make it clear that this wasn't for his mother, and even though he was rushing it, he knew without a doubt that he loved Claire and wanted to spend the rest of his life with her.

He pulled out the pouch. He didn't even want to look at it until he could ask Claire. He stuffed it in his front pocket. As quickly as he could, he packed his larger suitcase and made a beeline to Ace's car.

The entire ride to the airport, and subsequent flight, his heart fluttered, and his palms grew sweaty. His mind fast-forwarded to what he thought a life with her would be like.

When the limo pulled into the driveway of his

mother's house, the gravity of what he was about to do sucker-punched his ability to move. He sat in the back of the car feeling slightly nauseous, and a crushing pain slammed into his chest. For the last ten hours, he'd focused on the future and hadn't given a single thought as to how he would propose.

"I need to go to a florist right away," he told the driver.

CHAPTER 10

Claire stepped from the front door just as the limo pulled in. Gerry had told her that Hunter was on his way back, and she just wanted to set the record straight. That she was okay and that when enough time had passed, they could close the book in their fake reunion. But she wasn't going to get the chance because the limo backed up and drove away.

Hurt quickly turned to anger.

She stood outside, trying to control her raging pulse, but no amount of deep breathing would help, so she tried pacing in the front yard.

That only made it worse.

Fifteen minutes after the limo left, she stormed back into the house and slammed the door, rattling the painting on the wall.

"Claire," Judy said from the sitting room, tipping her head and glaring at her over her cheaters as she continued her knitting. "That was totally uncalled for."

Claire no longer cared what his family thought. "Hunter took one look at me and turned around and left." She pulled her phone from her back pocket and pulled up his contact information.

"I doubt that, dear."

"Well, that's what he did." She started to send a nasty text, but then decided he wasn't worth it if he couldn't even get out of the car and face her.

"What happened between the two of you?" Judy set her yarn on her lap.

"We found out the hard way that we aren't a good fit."

"Oh," Judy said, setting her glasses down. "I see."

"It doesn't matter and honestly, I think this actually gives us closure." She rubbed the back of her neck. "I'm going to get my things and head to my apartment."

"Wait until after dinner. Hunter's sister and brother will be here. I'm sure they will want to see you."

Both Emily and Miles had been supportive of Claire over the years, but she didn't need to be around them tonight. "It's really best if I go. It should just be immediate family right now."

"You're immediate family," Gerry said as he waltzed into the room.

"No. I'm not."

He rested his hand on her shoulder. "I really don't know happened, but I just got off the phone with Hunter. I told him you thought he left because of you and—"

"Mr. Thompson, why would you say that?" she screeched.

"Because I don't understand why you're so upset." He arched a brow. "He said he's sending the car back for you shortly."

"Why?" She looked at her phone and saw that Hunter had texted her twice and called three times. She pulled up the messages.

We need to talk. Sending car back for you.

Are you there? I've called and called. This is important. Please. Answer me.

The honking of a horn startled her.

"The car is here," Gerry said.

She swallowed, looking out the window at the stretch limo. The driver stood outside, his hand on the passenger rear door.

"Go," Judy said, waving her hand. "Whatever it is, don't you think you owe it to yourself to find out?"

"All right," she heard herself say.

She took slow tentative steps toward the vehicle. The driver opened the door, and she slipped inside, half wishing Hunter was inside so she could just get this over with and leave. "Where are we going?"

"I've been asked to take you to the club."

"The club? Why?"

"That's just what I was told."

She leaned back, folding her arms over her chest. Nothing made sense anymore. She wanted to go back to when she'd been given the choice to leave him on his boat. He said he would have come anyway, so that first night wouldn't have happened, and neither would have last night.

The ride to the club took all of ten minutes. She was greeted by a young bag boy in a golf cart.

"Mr. Jackson is waiting on the ninth green."

"Why?" She stared at the young boy who had the stupidest grin plastered on his face.

"I'm not at liberty to say."

As they rode across the golf course, the golfers stepped to the side, pointing and waving. They rolled down the eighth fairway and all she could think about was their first kiss, right there on the ninth green.

Her heart hammered against her chest. Through the trees, she saw Hunter standing at that very spot, roses in hand.

"Turn this sucker around," she whispered. The last time Hunter had given her roses was the first night they'd slept together. He hadn't done it since, saying that roses were only for the most special of occasions and then teased her that she wouldn't be getting them from him again unless he were to propose.

"Are you serious?" the bag boy asked with a high pitched squeak.

"Yes. No. I don't know," she muttered. No way could he be asking her that. Maybe he was just going to apologize for being an asshole. She could deal with that.

The kid pulled the cart up next to Hunter. The flowers in his hands shook.

"You made it," he said, holding out his hand.

She didn't take it. "What do you want, Hunter?"

Mentally, she beat the crap out of herself. Being a bitch wasn't going to help the situation.

"Do you remember what happened here?" he asked. His voice had a funny tone to it.

"Our first kiss."

"That was mind-blowing."

"I suppose," she said, pinching herself, trying to change her attitude. He was making an effort. The least she could do was meet him halfway.

"Are you mad at me?" he asked.

"Ya think?"

He scowled. "Whatever I did to upset you, I'm very sorry."

"You left without saying good-bye and went back to Florida."

"For an hour to get some—"

She held up her hand, painfully aware that a crowd of golfers had gathered in the distance. "You didn't wake me to tell me or leave me a note or even bother to text me. Considering our past history, what was I to think?"

"I left a note." He pinched his nose. "I said I'd be back."

"It felt like you snuck out after last night. I don't mind being used like that considering everything you're going through. I mean I offered myself up to you, but you could have done the decent thing and—"

He cupped her mouth.

She batted it away. "Don't hush me." She wasn't about to be quiet now. He hasn't really apologized for anything and didn't even understand why she was upset.

"You're yelling on a golf course, and people are starting to stare."

"You brought me here." She planted her hands on her hips.

"This isn't going as I planned." He scratched the side of his face. "Here. These are for you." He held out the roses, which trembled in his hands.

"Why are we here?" She took the roses, lifting them to her nose and inhaling the fresh scent.

"I had this whole thing planned to ask if you remembered our first kiss and the first time we..." He glanced around, and his cheeks flushed red.

She'd never seen him blush before. Ever.

"I remember the first time vividly," she whispered. Her throat dried up, and she could barely swallow.

"I gave you roses."

She nodded.

"Do you remember what I said about roses?"

"Oh my God. You can't be serious?" She reached out and clutched the nearest tree. "This is all just for show, right? For your mom, right? Give a dying woman her wish?"

"No."

"No?"

"I love you, Claire. I always have. I'm sorry that me racing off to get my mother's ring hurt you—"

"Ring?" She dropped the flowers. Her muscles felt like jelly. "What ring?

"My mother's ring," he said.

"Why do you have your mother's ring? What kind of ring does your mother have?"

"An engagement ring, and she sent it to me years ago. I don't know why I kept it. I thought about sending it back to her, but never did."

"This isn't happening," she whispered, staring into his smoldering eyes.

"Do you love me back, Claire?"

Without thinking, she nodded.

He lowered himself to one knee.

She clutched her necklace, staring down at him holding out a diamond—a huge diamond ring.

"The second you stepped onto my boat, I couldn't deny any more how much I missed you. I'm not going to give you any kind of ultimatum. I can be a firefighter anywhere. It doesn't have to be in the Air Force."

"You can't give that up for me."

"I can and I will, if you shoot me down today." He took her hand and dropped his forehead to it. "Which I hope you don't, but I will stick it out and fight for us this time."

"You're really asking me to marry you?" A wide smile tugged at the corners of her mouth. Her heart fluttered, and she felt like she was floating on air.

"Yes."

"That's my line," she said.

He slipped the ring on her finger and kissed her hand. "Is that a yes?"

"Can I think about it?"

He stood, taking her into his strong, protective arms. "You're killing me here."

"I love you, Hunter Jackson, and I'm never going to let you go." She pressed her lips against his, listening to the cheers in the background.

"I love you," he whispered in ear. "I have one more thing to ask you."

"What's that?"

"Can we get married right away. I know you probably want the white dress, big wedding—"

"We can get a marriage license tomorrow and

since this is because you want your mother there, I'm sure she'd let us have a small ceremony at the house."

A golfer in the distance yelled four.

They climbed up on the back of the golf cart. "I'm not letting you leave the Air Force."

"Well, I can't leave right away. I've got two years left, but I don't know if I'd re-enlist. It's a hard life for a family."

"But one I readily accept." She bit down on her lower lip. "We were careless last night."

He shrugged. "We're not getting any younger."

EPILOGUE

Two years later...

Hunter pushed back the garage door to the home he and Claire had bought not far from the base. He'd made the decision to stay with the Air Force, and he fulfilled his dream to be an arson investigator. His deployments would be minimal, especially now that they had little Annabelle Louisa. His heart physically hurt just thinking about leaving her for any length of time.

Being at work during the day was hard enough.

"I hear Daddy," Claire cooed.

"Da Da," Annabelle screamed as she wobbled

down the hallway, her hands flapping in the air. At fifteen months, she was an inquisitive ball of energy.

"How's my baby girl?" He bent over and scooped her into his arms, brushing away her long blonde locks, just like her mother.

"Good." She cupped his face with her pudgy little hands and pursed her lips. "Mommy had bad day."

"Oh no, what's happened?" Claire had made the decision to create her own foundation to help create safe environments for women and children who suffered abuse. This had been a huge undertaking, but the millions of dollars they had between both families wasn't doing anyone any good sitting in some stock or bond.

"Mommy sick!"

"Then we best get inside and help her out tonight." He set Annabelle down, who went running off into the family room, bouncing twice off the walls, giggling all the way. She jumped on the sofa where Claire had stretched out her legs.

"Hey, babe, what's going on?"

"Not dinner," she said with a weak smile.

"I think I can handle cooking tonight. Did you have something in mind?"

"I took out chicken, but when I was preparing it, I barfed."

"Stay away from me, then. Last thing I need is the stomach bug."

"You can't get this kind of ailment," she said, shifting to a sitting position. "Annabelle, will you go get Mommy the crackers?"

"All sicknesses are contagious." He sat down next to the woman that would forever rock his world, pressing the back of his hand on her cheek, but she didn't feel warm.

"Morning sickness is not contagious."

"Ha ha. It's evening and...no." He dropped his hand to his thigh. "You're pregnant?"

She nodded. "I took the test this morning when the smell of coffee made me want to puke my guts out."

"We're going to have another kid?" He pointed to Annabelle, who handed Claire a sleeve of saltines. "Two of those little things?"

Annabelle jumped up on his lap. "What little things, Da Da?"

"Mommy's going to have a baby." Tears stung the corners of his eyes.

"Yay!" She kissed his lips before jumping down

and running off toward her toys in the middle of the room. The kid couldn't sit still for a second.

He looped his arm around Claire, pulling her close. "I'm sorry our babies make you sick."

"It's only for a few months," she said, smiling. "I'm more concerned about how you're going to be when she starts dating."

"I'll be fine, because she won't be allowed to date. Ever. No boy is going to try to kiss my little girl."

"Because she's going to take after her mother and kiss them first."

The End

ABOUT THE AUTHOR

Jen Talty is an award-winning author of Romantic Suspense. Dark Water hit #10 in Barnes and Noble and her books have been in the top 50 on Amazon. Jennifer grew up in Rochester, New York. She recently retired from being a full-time hockey mom as her children hung up their skates. She and her husband still live in Rochester while her children travel globe. Jen was the co-founder of Cool Gus Publishing with NY Times Bestselling Author Bob Mayer.

Sign up for Jen's Newsletter where she often gives away free books before publication.
Join Jen's private Facebook group where she posts exclusive excerpts and discuss all things murder and love!

BB bookbub.com/authors/jen-talty

ALSO BY JEN TALTY

SPECIAL FORCES: OPERATION ALPHA:

FIRE PROTECTION SPECIALISTS

Burning Desire

Burning Kiss

Burning Skies

Burning Lies

The New York State Trooper Series

In Two Weeks

Dark Water

Deadly Secrets

Murder in Paradise Bay

To Protect His Own

Deadly Seduction

When a Stranger Calls

Federal Investigator Series

Jane Doe's Return

The Butterfly Murders

THE MEN OF THEIF LAKE

Rekindled

THE OMEGA TEAM: THE SARICH BROTHERS

The Lighthouse

Her Last Hope

The Last Flight

The Phoenix Agency: The Raven Sisters

The Lost Sister

The Lost Solider

The Brotherhood Protectors: Out Of The Wild

Rough Justice

Paranormal Dating Agency

The Blind Date

Spring Fling

Sassy Ever After

Lady Sass

All That Sass

Federal Investigator Series

Jane Doe's Return

Imagine spending your entire career looking for the one person you believe will unlock the mystery of who killed your sister only to find her the most unlikely place; in your office, as your new partner. Special Agent Travis Brown has set his life up so he can have access to information that will lead him to the one woman he believes can tell him who killed his sister. But he's not prepared for the drive and determination of his new partner; Special Agent Shauna Morgan. Her instincts are sharp and her beauty undeniable. His attraction to her is as strong as his need to find his sister's killer. But Shauna has a secret. A secret that will ultimately put his heart on the line, along with her life. Jane Doe's Return is a contemporary romantic suspense set between the city streets of Albany, New York and the scenic beauty of Lake George where I lived for many years. It is a tale of one woman who believes the only way to move beyond her past, is to shut the door on it, and the man who breaks it down. Jane Doe's Return is the recipient of The Molly and The Beacon Romance Writing Contests.

The Butterfly Murders

Special Agent Kara Martin has spent the last thirteen years doing whatever she could to obliterate memories of her hometown...and haunting reminders of her parents' murders. She had every intent of avoiding Rochester... until a congressman's daughter is murdered, and she finds herself not only back to a place she said she'd never return, but working with a man she thought she'd never see again.

A man who once loved her... until she broke his heart.

Detective Shane Rogers lost his wife and a year later nearly lost his son when his rare heart condition took a turn for the worst. Battling back from personal devastation, his son is now thriving after a successful heart transplant and Shane can finally return to his second love...his career as a homicide detective.

His first case is the gruesome murder of a local congressman's fourteen-year-old daughter, bringing in the FBI and putting Shane face to face with his first love.

Shane and Kara are thrust together in one of the toughest cases of their careers while pieces of their pasts crop up to taunt them.

As they begin to face their pasts and find forgiveness, the bodies pile up. With each new murder, the killer takes a different organ that is commonly harvested. An organ they had received in the form of a transplant.

And now Shane's son has been kidnapped...

The New York State Trooper Series

In Two Weeks

(New York State Trooper Series Book 1)

Ryan O'Conner has the world at her fingertips. She's strong, feisty and has everything she's ever wanted, except the right man. Jared Blake represents everything Ryan doesn't want. He's controlling, overbearing and now he's moving. Having had a crush on him for years, Ryan decides to seduce Jared. A goodbye thing. However, her plans change when someone starts stalking her. With her life on the line, she turns to Jared for protection and finds the not so perfect man is the perfect man for her.

Restless and bored, NY State Trooper Jared Blake accepts a transfer from his position in Lake George, NY. Jared craves the rush of adrenaline and his current post is too tame. As soon as he moves, his career will take off, but his plans are put on hold when a friend is threatened by a stalker. Jared has exactly two weeks to find out who is behind these treats.

And in two weeks, Jared will lose his heart forever...

Dark Water

(New York State Trooper Series Book 2)

Lacy DeGeorgio never imagined she'd have to be responsible for anyone but herself. She's strong, stubborn and fiercely independent. She needs no one. She's a woman determined to do things her way, on her own. But when a freak boating accident takes her sister Hannah's life, Lacy finds herself not only back in her hometown of Lake George, New York, but in a custody battle for her eleven-year-old nephew, Andy. Just when things couldn't get any worse, pesky State Trooper Frank Harmon starts showing up, tearing down all her defenses, making her want things she's never wanted before. She'll trust him with her nephew, but can she trust him with her heart?

New York State Trooper Frank Harmon is a man of honor and duty. He's always done things by the book, believing the law always works in favor of those who uphold it.

Until the day he took a domestic disturbance call at the DeGeorgio trailer, and even though he knew something bad was about to happen, he had to walk away. Two days later, he pulled Hannah DeGeorgio's body from the icy cold waters of Lake George, changing his life forever. He sets out to make sure Hannah's killer is brought to justice and in the process makes a home for a family he thought he never wanted.

Deadly Secrets

(New York State Trooper Series Book 3)

After staring down the wrong end of a gun, not once, but twice, all Patty Harmon had wanted was to have a little fun. She'd spent most her life taking care of everyone else but herself. And while she had a plan for her life, she hadn't yet started to live her life. So, when the aloof, distant, and emotionally unavailable New York State Trooper Reese McGinn takes an interest in her, she's all in...for the moment. When the moment is over, they go their separate ways and Patty can get back to her life plan. But once again, that plan is interrupted when Patty finds herself pregnant. She'll let Reese back in for the sake of the child, but can she keep Reese from stealing her heart?

New York State Trooper Reese McGinn has been haunted

by his late mothers confession and the secret she still took to her grave. For the last seven years, he's done nothing but move from job to job and town to town, vowing to never put down roots. But when his summer fling with Patty Harmon ends with a child on the way, he decides that its time to forget the past. Only the past doesn't want to forge him and a deadly secret rises from the grave, threatening to take away everything he thought he never wanted.

Murder in Paradise Bay

(New York State Trooper Series Book 4)

Things were finally looking up for Douglas Tanner. His divorce was about to be final. His construction company was doing better than ever and he was ready to start a new beginning. He just hadn't expected that new beginning included his long time friend and daughter of his business partner. But just as he expresses his new found feelings for Stacey, his soon to be ex-wife is found dead in the bottom of Lake George one day before he was to sign the divorce papers.

And Doug is the prime suspect. Not just in his wife's murder. But also her lover's disappearance.

New York State Trooper Stacey Sutten had just finished

her rescue swimmer certification course and finally had some time to relax. Or so she thought as she's called to a search and rescue mission. Only there was no rescue and the body she found just happened to be the wife of the man she was falling in love with.

As Doug and Stacey's romance heats up, so does the case. One damning piece of evidence after the other lead the police to Doug's door. Caught between trying to prove Doug's innocent and doing her job, Stacey finds herself in the hot seat. Just when she thinks it can't get any worse, she's investigated as a possible accomplice.

Stacey must find out who really killed Mary, why they are hell bent on framing herself and the man she loves, before both of them get good look at the inside of a jail cell.

THE MEN OF THEIF LAKE

Rekindled

For the last nine years, Kaylee Mead has been running from her past. Now she's running for her life. Her only chance at survival is to return home and patch things up with her father. When she returns to her home in Thief

Lake, Minnesota, she finds her father dead and herself becoming the cop's best suspect for his murder. Assistant Police Chief Blaine Walker has been trying to put his ex-wife out of his mind for years, but when he finds her hovered over her father's body, he knows that battle is lost. She becomes his only suspect in a case that doesn't make sense. He vows to find the answers and then hopefully rekindle the flame that has never quite died out in his heart.

As you know, this book included at least one character from Susan Stoker's books. To check out more, see below.

Delta Force Heroes Series

Rescuing Rayne (FREE!)

Rescuing Aimee (novella)

Rescuing Emily

Rescuing Harley

Marrying Emily

Rescuing Kassie

Rescuing Bryn

Rescuing Casey

Rescuing Sadie

Rescuing Wendy

Rescuing Mary (Oct 2018)

Rescuing Macie (April 2019)

Badge of Honor: Texas Heroes Series

Justice for Mackenzie (FREE!)

Justice for Mickie

Justice for Corrie

Justice for Laine (novella)

Shelter for Elizabeth

Justice for Boone

Shelter for Adeline

Shelter for Sophie

Justice for Erin

Justice for Milena

Shelter for Blythe

Justice for Hope (Sept 2018)

Shelter for Quinn (Feb 2019)

Shelter for Koren (June 2019)

Shelter for Penelope (Oct 2019)

SEAL of Protection Series

Protecting Caroline (FREE!)

Protecting Alabama

Protecting Fiona

Marrying Caroline (novella)

Protecting Summer

Protecting Cheyenne

Protecting Jessyka

Protecting Julie (novella)

Protecting Melody

Protecting the Future

Protecting Kiera (novella)

Protecting Dakota

SEAL of Protection: Legacy Series

Securing Caite (Jan 2019)

Securing Sidney (May 2019)
Securing Piper (Sept 2019)
Securing Zoey (TBA)
Securing Avery (TBA)
Securing Kalee (TBA)

New York Times, *USA Today* and *Wall Street Journal* Bestselling Author Susan Stoker has a heart as big as the state of Texas where she lives, but this all American girl has also spent the last fourteen years living in Missouri, California, Colorado, and Indiana. She's married to a retired Army man who now gets to follow *her* around the country.

She debuted her first series in 2014 and quickly followed that up with the SEAL of Protection Series, which solidified her love of writing and creating stories readers can get lost in.

If you enjoyed this book, or any book, please consider leaving a review. It's appreciated by authors more than you'll know.

www.stokeraces.com
www.AcesPress.com
susan@stokeraces.com

More Books in the Special Forces: Operation Alpha World!

Brynne Asher: Blackburn
Denise Agnew: Dangerous to Hold
Shauna Allen: Awakening Aubrey
Shauna Allen: Defending Danielle
Shauna Allen: Rescuing Rebekah
Shauna Allen: Saving Scarlett
Shauna Allen: Saving Grace
Jennifer Becker: Hiding Catherine
Julia Bright: Saving Lorelei
Victoria Bright: Surviving Savage
Victoria Bright: Going Ghost
Victoria Bright: Jostling Joker
Kendra Mei Chailyn: Beast
Kendra Mei Chailyn: Barbie
Kendra Mei Chailyn : Pitbull
Melissa Kay Clarke: Rescuing Annabeth
Melissa Kay Clarke: Safeguarding Miley
Samantha A. Cole: Handling Haven
Samantha A. Cole: Cheating the Devil
Sue Coletta: Hacked
KaLyn Cooper: Rescuing Melina
Liz Crowe: Marking Mariah

Jordan Dane: Redemption for Avery
Jordan Dane: Fiona's Salvation
Riley Edwards: Protecting Olivia
Riley Edwards: Redeeming Violet
Nicole Flockton: Protecting Maria
Nicole Flockton: Guarding Erin
Nicole Flockton: Guarding Suzie
Nicole Flockton: Guarding Brielle
Casey Hagen: Shielding Nebraska
Casey Hagen: Shielding Harlow
Casey Hagen: Shielding Josie
Desiree Holt: Protecting Maddie
Kathy Ivan: Saving Sarah
Kathy Ivan: Saving Savannah
Kathy Ivan: Saving Stephanie
Jesse Jacobson: Protecting Honor
Jesse Jacobson: Fighting for Honor
Jesse Jacobson: Defending Honor
Jesse Jacobson: Summer Breeze
Silver James: Rescue Moon
Silver James: SEAL Moon
Silver James: Assassin's Moon
Becca Jameson: Saving Sofia
Kate Kinsley: Protecting Ava
Heather Long: Securing Arizona
Heather Long: Guarding Gertrude

Heather Long: Protecting Pilar

Heather Long: Covering Coco

Kirsten Lynn: Joining Forces for Jesse

Margaret Madigan: Bang for the Buck

Margaret Madigan: Buck the System

Margaret Madigan: Jungle Buck

Margaret Madigan: December Chill

Rachel McNeely: The SEAL's Surprise Baby

Rachel McNeely: The SEAL's Surprise Bride

KD Michaels: Saving Laura

KD Michaels: Protecting Shane

Wren Michaels: The Fox & The Hound

Wren Michaels: The Fox & The Hound 2

Wren Michaels: Shadow of Doubt

Wren Michaels: Shift of Fate

Wren Michaels: Steeling His Heart

Kat Mizera: Protecting Bobbi

Mary B Moore: Force Protection

LeTeisha Newton: Protecting Butterfly

LeTeisha Newton: Protecting Goddess

LeTeisha Newton: Protecting Vixen

LeTeisha Newton: Protecting Heartbeat

MJ Nightingale: Protecting Beauty

MJ Nightingale: Betting on Benny

MJ Nightingale: Protecting Secrets

Sarah O'Rourke: Saving Liberty

Made in the USA
Monee, IL
18 February 2020

21989568R00089